LOVE ME, IF YOU DARE

BOOK 1: WAGERS AND WALLFLOWERS

ALYSSA CLARKE

First Edition February 2021

Edited by AuthorsDesigns and Gina Fiserova
Proofread by Theresa McGregor
Cover design and formatting by AuthorsDesigns.

For my family who rooted for me to write this series! For my amazing husband, who did all the cooking while I burrowed in the writing hut.

Wagers and Wallflowers series

Love me, if you dare
Marry me, if you Dare
Seduce me, if you Dare
Ruin me, if you Dare
Kiss me, if you Dare
Tempt me, if you Dare

CHAPTER ONE

*T*he afternoon sun receded as bloated gray clouds scuttled across the sky. The scent of wild earth permeated the air, and a cool gust of wind flapped the golden drapes by the open windows. It was unusual to have such dreary weather in spring, Sebastian George Crawford, the Duke of Hartford idly noted, quietly thankful for the mercurial nature of the weather. The unexpected shift from bright and merry to an overcast sky perfectly suited his quiet contemplation as he stood in his office facing his sister, who had just returned from her excursion.

Three little lies.

Separately they might be considered unimportant, such small fibs they were not worthy of any attention. However, once combined, they were the sum of many older brother's fears, especially for one who had permitted his younger sister to do one of the most dangerous things required of them at this tender age—debut into the marriage mart of London's society.

In the marriage mart, the true underbelly of the *ton*, if a debutante was not properly chaperoned, she might encounter a rake…a libertine who might encourage her into a ruinous scandal with seductive whispers and touches.

Except his sister, Lady Perdita, should have been safe. For she was already engaged to a young gentleman whom she loved with her entire heart and soul. Or so she had prettily assured Sebastian when she had begged him to allow their engagement.

Those three little lies—a headache to escape early from a ball but not returning home until hours after, an afternoon trek to the milliner but going elsewhere, and now this…

"So, you had a lovely walk in the park," Sebastian said in a smooth, unconcerned tone, not at all liking the hard knot in his gut.

He turned to face her, noting the rising rosy pink in her softly rounded cheeks. He had truly thought her safe from unwanted advances, given her close attachment to the young viscount. The flush on her cheeks and that quick, unfathomable glitter in her expressive grey-blue eyes made her an enigma to Sebastian, for why else would she need to lie?

"Yes, the walk in Hyde Park was perfectly wonderful," Perdie said, tugging at the strings to her bonnet, flashing him her warmest smile. "I had a most relaxing time."

Sebastian did a credible job in masking the alarm darting through his heart upon once again hearing his sister and apple of his eyes lie to him so smoothly. Grown men, powerful lords, and those with whom he had business dealing wouldn't dare. Or if they attempted it, surely they would not manage that level of composure. His sister didn't shift uncomfortably, nor did her eyes skitter away with guilt. This informed him Perdie was becoming practiced and very much at ease in the art of deflection. Why it was necessary befuddled him, and with a small jolt, Sebastian admitted it hurt.

"Perdie," he began gruffly. "You do know you can speak with me about anything?"

A soft breath shuddered through his sister, and she was careful in not meeting his eyes.

"Of course, how odd that you would say so, brother."

As if to reassure him all was well, she hurried toward him, rose onto her toes, and placed an affectionate kiss on his cheek. "If you do not mind, Seb, I will skip our afternoon tea and chat. Will you please let mama know I am going to take a nap in preparation for tonight's ball. The walk tired me more than I imagined it would."

A whisper of warning sizzled along his nape. "Lord Owen called earlier."

While turning away from him, Perdie froze. "Oh?"

"Yes. It seemed there had been plans for him to take you out in his new barouche. The weather was delightful, and there was much to talk about."

Without facing him, his sister replied, "Oh dear, I must have forgotten! How clumsy of me. I shall send him a note of apology and save two dances for him tonight at Lady Edgecombe's ball."

Sebastian considered the stiffness of her posture. "When I told Lord Owen you were not here, he made his way to Hyde Park. I was surprised when he returned a couple hours later saying he did not see you there, and he had made a round of the park."

A fine tremor went through her elegant frame, and Sebastian took a few steps closer to her, not liking the odd feeling twisting deep in his insides.

"Perdie?"

She turned to him, lifting her chin high, her expression carefully composed. Her lips flattened, and an emotion he could not identify flashed across her eyes. "The park must have been too crowded. As a gentleman, he should have simply arranged for another outing, not stalk me to the park. How positively medieval of him."

"He was not stalking you," Sebastian said mildly, masking his surprise at that acerbic reply.

"Lord Owen is your fiancé. Even I thought it proper for him to head to Hyde Park in the hopes of seeing you."

"And because he is my fiancé, I am not allowed the freedom to walk with my companion alone?"

"Of course not, Perdie." Sebastian casually sat on the edge of his desk. "Did you and Lord Owen have a falling out? You seem very out of sorts with the viscount."

Lord Owen had acted like a fool earlier, ranting that he had lost her love and attention. Sebastian had given him a stern lecture and sent him home.

"We did not quarrel," Perdie said softly, heading toward the door. "I just recalled I have some correspondence to deal with. I shall attend to it and then take my rest."

"You can confide in me about anything," he said. The discomfort in his gut grew until it spread through his entire body. Sebastian couldn't pinpoint exactly when his sister had started to change. The change was infinitesimal, but it was there. They had not lied to each other, *ever*, and yet she had done so with such ease. "Perdie, were you at Hyde Park?"

Her gloved hand tightened on the doorknob. "Where else would I have been?"

Then she opened the door and sallied outside, closing it behind her.

Sebastian stared at that closed door, waiting to see if she would return, tip her head, and laugh in that charmingly unfettered way of hers before admitting she had been elsewhere. The door opened, but it was his mother, the Duchess of Hartford, who entered, fashionably dressed in a dark green riding habit of the latest style, a hat with several plume feathers tilted rakishly atop her mahogany brown curls. At five and fifty, his mother appeared to be a lady ten years younger and owned an even younger lady's energy.

"Perdie has returned home?" she asked, tugging her gloves from her hands.

"I wasn't aware she had been missing," he said drily.

No, his sister had been very circumspect in the address she had scurried off to for almost three hours. And then lied about it. *Bloody hell*. This was a scandal waiting to happen, and he did not want that for her or their family.

"Anna mentioned that she was missing," his mother said, taking off her hat and fluffing the feathers, before tossing it onto the sofa closest to her.

Mrs. Anna Harrington was a young lady of modest means who served as his mother's companion. She was also a busy body who loved to gossip. Mrs. Harrington's daughter Miss Felicity acted as friend and chaperone to his sister, and they were often in each other's pocket. So whatever Perdie was about, he was perfectly sure that Miss Felicity knew it.

"Your daughter was not missing. She claimed to have been in Hyde Park with Miss Felicity."

His mother arched an elegant brow. "I've been down Rotten Row and around the Serpentine at least three times catching up on the latest *on dit* with Lady Ambury and Lady Landish. I did not see Perdie."

"I know she was not there."

The implications behind his words robbed the breath from his mother, and she slowly sat in the well-padded armchair by the low burning fire. "Perdie lied about her whereabouts?"

"Yes."

His mother's hand fluttered to her chest. "Are you certain, Sebastian?"

"Yes."

"I do not believe it."

"Your daughter left under the guise of going to the park, but she was somewhere else entirely."

A touch of alarm entered his mother's bright blue eyes. "Why would Perdie act in such a careless manner? And how did you come to know of it?"

"Lord Owen called earlier. They had arranged to ride in his new barouche," Sebastian said, walking over to an armchair and sitting down. Quickly he relayed the tale of his sister's fiancé heading to the park and returning to their townhouse flustered and flummoxed.

"How dare he harbor such suspicions about Perdie," the duchess snapped. "They have been betrothed for two years, and their wedding is only three months away. What nonsense is he thinking about losing her affection to another? Who else might he say such nonsense to?"

"That is why I took it upon myself to sternly question the coachman as to where he has been taking Perdie." Sebastian shook his head, almost amused at her daring. "For the last few weeks, she has been visiting a particular townhouse in Berkeley Square. Thankfully, Miss Felicity always accompanies her, but Perdie bribed the coachman to keep his silence whenever she takes the carriage. And as the servants are fond of her, he was persuaded to go along with her request. He was very reluctant to reveal the information, but I reminded him who pays his wages."

Sebastian felt a rush of sympathy for his mother, whose face had paled alarmingly.

"I beg your pardon?" The duchess's voice was a mere whisper, and in her eyes, he spied fright and outrage. "My daughter would not act in any salacious manner to ruin this family's good name and reputation."

An edgy restlessness bit at Sebastian's bones. "We do not know whose house it is," he gently reminded her, though Sebastian himself did not believe it to be innocent. If it were above scrutiny, there would have been no need for his sister to lie about her whereabouts or to bribe their coachman to secrecy for the last few weeks. He had given her every opportunity to tell the truth.

"Does it matter whose townhouse it is? Surely it cannot be something good or respectable. Dear Lord in heaven, what was she thinking?"

Sebastian was familiar with the less than civilized workings of the male mind, yet as for a lady's thoughts, he believed navigating a battlefield littered with traps might be easier. He didn't know his sister's thoughts or what she might be going through at this very moment, and that frightened Sebastian immensely. And he was not a man easily rattled. He was a duke and had been so from the tender age of nineteen. He had been more than Perdie's brother; he had become practically her father and confidant. However, Sebastian could sense her pulling from him, and the helpless feelings worming through his heart could not be tolerated.

In his mother's eyes, he spotted a similar fear. And the promise to fix everything rose unswerving inside him. His duty was always to his family, one he had accepted with pride, love, and honor. "You need not worry, madam; I will get to the heart of this matter concerning Perdie."

His mother shook her head a bit dazedly. "Where is she now? I will demand an explanation."

"I do not want her to be aware of our knowledge."

His mother stood. "You still think of her sensibilities when you should—"

"Mother, I cannot guess at Perdie's thinking at the moment. I do not dare confront her because I must know who is at that townhouse and what we need to prepare for. Perdie can be very obstinate. I do not want her to warn the bounder, allowing him to run."

The duchess closed her eyes, her expression pained. "I am thinking of all the times she has been from our sight. It…it truly cannot be contemplated."

It seemed his mother had drawn a similar conclusion. That whoever his sister stole away to visit during the day and even last week when she begged to leave a ball early pleading a headache. He feared it was all to visit this particular house.

"How often does she visit this…place?" the duchess whispered.

"At least three times a week for the past month."

"And we have not noticed? Though she is affianced and allowed liberties not afforded to other debutantes, she is always properly chaperoned with Miss Felicity as her companion!" His mother's expression cleared, and her lips flattened. "Of course, Perdie has convinced Miss Felicity to deceive us in this willful and insupportable manner! Lord Owen must never find out about this, Sebastian. He loves Perdie very much, and he is from a fine, upstanding family. Should he discover her activities—"

His mother placed a gloved hand over her

mouth as if she couldn't bear to say whatever fear lingered in her heart. That her daughter had led herself to be seduced and ruined.

"Perdie has good sense," Sebastian reassured his mother, masking his own turmoil and the rage bubbling deep within him. Whoever had preyed upon his sister would rue the day they initiated the scheme. "I am certain she has not allowed herself to be wayward. Perhaps it is not what we think."

His mother sent him a glance filled with fury and disappointment.

"I will hold my tongue until you uncover what this is all about."

"You have my word I will not delay. Do not expect me at Lady Edgecombe's ball this evening. Do pay close attention to Perdie."

The duchess nodded. "Do you plan…plan to visit that house today?"

"I sent word to my man of affairs to uncover who owns or occupies that townhouse. He should have the information by tomorrow. I shall, however, not delay in my visit."

His mother took a few bracing breaths, and it pained him to see the worry in her eyes. It was an emotion he felt in his heart, for he could not imagine what sort of shenanigans his young, innocent sister might have embroiled herself.

"The scandal—"

"Let's not get ahead of ourselves. We do not

know what I will find in that house. It might be innocent."

"You are a man of the world," his mother snapped. "Surely you do not believe that nonsense. The recklessness of her scheme could make life exceedingly difficult for both of you. You might be a duke, a very wealthy one, but even your reputation matters. Our family's reputation matters. If this gets out, you might lose your opportunity to match with Lady Edith."

He stared at his mother, almost admiring the manipulative ease in which she had slipped that lady's name into the conversation. "I see you've been sucked into the assumptions of everyone else in the *ton* into thinking I intend to offer for Lady Edith."

There was even a wager on it at White's; it had got as far as to be written in the book that he would offer for Lady Edith this month or closer to the end of the season. Serious money would be lost if he did not propose. He had laughed somewhat bitterly in annoyance when he'd heard of the entry.

His mother shot him a startled glance at his cold tone. "Is there anyone else you wish to marry in society? I cannot imagine anyone else who would be a better match for you. She would make the perfect duchess for you. The daughter of a marquess, she's a very accomplished dancer and speaks three languages fluently. Surely, you must realize she was the only eligible young lady you danced with last season. It was all anyone talked about for weeks."

"It wasn't a marriage offer," he said with simplicity. "It was a dance."

"There was nothing simple about it. Lady Edith is known to have rejected several splendid offers for her hand, and I suspect we both know who she is waiting upon."

"I do hope it is not me!"

"Of course, it is you!"

Though he had overheard sly hints on many lips that he had found his duchess, at last, he was far from convinced. Lady Edith was indeed beautiful and openly had been declared incomparable these last three seasons. She was also a witty conversationalist, and he had liked that she hadn't tried to hide her intelligence when they had conversed.

"I have not given her any encouragement…"

His mother laughed, something mocking in her eyes piercing him. "You are thirty, my dear, and I sense the shift in your moods of late. You are thinking of settling down and filling your nursery with the patter of little feet. And I happened to come across your list, so I am perfectly aware Lady Edith is at the very top of it."

Bloody hell. He had made a list of all the eligible ladies currently out in society. Sebastian should have known the current duchess would have snooped to uncover it. Now he understood why the duchess had expended so little effort over the past few weeks in reminding him of his duty to his title and the realm. "If you will excuse me, madam, I will prepare to pay a visit to Berkeley Square."

"To turn up without any warning will be a great shock for the reprobate. I highly doubt you will be admitted."

"I am the Duke of Hartford, who dares turn me away?"

CHAPTER TWO

Four hours earlier…

*L*aughter—light, tinkling, and unfettered, filtered through the doors and hallways of one particular townhouse at 48 Berkeley Square. Lady Theodosia Winfern—Theo to her friends and family—sauntered down the second-floor hallway, her feet bare of shoes and stockings, her mass of golden-brown hair rippling down her shoulders to settle at her lower back. Her mimosa muslin gown rumpled and slightly grubby. It was a cute confection, with the satin stripes of the same color in the weave and accented by a profusion of ribbon knots in a glowing daffodil yellow.

Merriment spilled through an open door, beckoning her closer. Theo paused at the entrance, a smile touching her mouth at the sight of five ladies sprawled indecorously onto the carpet before a fire, playing cards. Their bonnets had been discarded, their elaborate coiffures unpinned, shoes kicked off their feet, all pretentious airs of perfect ladylike decorum left on the doorstep leading to this townhouse. When they leave, they would again cloak themselves in perfect respectability. They would appear exactly how society and their families imagined they should be—demure, biddable, the faultless pictures of propriety.

"We have toppled the queen," Lady Anna squealed, throwing her hands in the air, uncaring the cards took flight from her elegant and gloveless fingers before settling all around on the blue Aubusson carpet.

"You cheat!" Lady Judith cried to her friends, tossing her cards on the carpet, pouting that she had lost. "You have all colluded against me, I can tell!"

The other ladies did not take her poor sportsmanship to heart, instead finding humor in her defeat. Soon Judith chuckled sheepishly before challenging them to another round of cards. A healthy wager even started, with Lady Elizabeth jumping to her feet and hurrying to the small table to gather papers and an inkwell to record their wager.

Theo chuckled and moved on to the other open door, where this time grunts of effort and the clinks of swords rang. Their resident fencing and archery master, Monsieur Jean-Phillipe Lambert, shuffled forward with lithe grace as he parried Lady Francie's advance.

Initially, Theo hadn't thought to teach the members of her society the art of self-defense. However, at a ball a few months ago, she had come upon Miss Carlisle sobbing her heart out in the gardens, the shoulder of her gown torn.

A cad had assaulted her, all with the intention of compromising her honor and reputation so she might be forced to marry him. The helplessness in her gaze had filled Theo with such anger she had hurriedly bundled the young lady away to a more private area and arranged her clothes in proper order. Then she had spent several minutes teaching her how to form a fist and exactly how she should use it if another bounder dared to accost her person.

She had become inspired to add teaching her ladies fencing and the art of boxing as another pursuit to partake in. Many ladies were already allowed these sports as a gentle exercise, but Theo allowed for a much more serious pursuit under her roof.

The room was empty and saved for the pair, and they were so concentrated on their fight, Theo did not linger. This was one of her favorite times of the day, walking the hall and checking on her members. A dozen large rooms spread over the second and third floor, which had all been converted into intimate, warm, and inviting spaces for the ladies of Theo's club. The first floor and its rooms were the larger common areas that tended to be less populated during the daytime.

A sense of accomplishment and joy always filled her soul to know she provided such a calming and enjoyable respite to so many ladies. They were more than members of her club; they felt like a sisterhood, a family which stood in place of the one she'd never had. She had formed many friendships with the girls, acting more in the capacity of an older sister than anything else. There were a few members older than Theo's six and twenty, and in them, she found a different sort of companionship. They were the older sisters and aunts to her and had become her closest of friends.

A forlorn sigh had her peeking through a half ajar door. A young girl, one of Theo's newest members, sat close to the windows overlooking the gardens, her elbows resting on the sill. Though she wore a yellow dress that accentuated her slim figure, its brightness giving her a gay and buxom appearance, an air of unhappiness hovered about her. Theo's heart squeezed. The girl presented a lovely tableau. Her wistful pose struck so naturally; the window framing the picture of her clad in a too innocent ivory frock, so demure that she might have been intended to enter a nunnery. Her peaches and cream complexion marred only by the distress revealed in her eyes.

The reason she'd created this place and worked

so hard for it to be a success was for somewhere ladies of the *ton* who were damn near forced to be perfect in everything could have a safe place where they could be themselves without fear of judgment or reproach. Each member was urged to leave all the cares of society expectation behind once they crossed the threshold to this townhouse and simply be free.

Theo knocked gently, and the girl whipped her head around. It was indeed Lady Perdita, and she had been crying. She hurriedly wiped the tears from her face and smiled. Her lips trembled before she firmed them and lifted her chin.

"Lady Theo," she said, jumping to her feet and dipping into a curtsy.

"You know we do not stand on formality here, Perdie," she said gently and made her way into the private sitting area, tastefully furnished with only a few pieces of silver chased furniture; a chaise longue, two high wingback chairs, and an ottoman, all upholstered in rich shades of purple and lilac. The openness tended to create a more relaxing space for the ladies, and each room had been designed to be spacious and welcoming. Theo did not sit but padded over to Lady Perdita.

"Shall I ring for some tea?"

A small laugh hiccupped from Perdita, and even with her eyes red from crying, she was ravishingly beautiful. "I've heard that you solve *everything* over tea. I never believed it before until now."

Theo smiled. "I gather the ladies discussed my belief in the curative wonders of tea."

"At times, they mention the whisky as well."

Theo laughed. "That is reserved for the most nerve-wracking times. I sense all my secrets are being spilled."

"Oh, yes, you are very admired and loved," Perdie murmured, glancing away.

That sense of warmth rushed through Theo once again. "There are only thirty-seven of us at the moment, but I would like to hope we have a special sort of sisterhood we can trust and rely on."

The young girl smiled. "Is that an invitation to confide in you of my troubles?"

"Only if you believe I might be of help to you, and only if it will help ease the burden I can see settled so heavily on your shoulders."

Those slim shoulders stiffened, and her throat worked on a swallow. "I've only been a member of your club for six weeks," she said hoarsely. "And it is everything…*everything* I could have hoped for in a lady's club. I've met so many wonderful ladies whom I might not have spoken with at a social outing."

Theo frowned. Only ladies from the *ton* were members of her club. She dared not be too liberal in whom she allowed membership as she had to care for the reputations of the ladies who entrusted themselves to her. Despite the prominence of their families and connections, several of her ladies felt they were outcasts because society called them wallflowers and bluestockings. It was rare for her to admit a debutante to their club, but Theo had allowed a few to join them after conducting informal interviews. Most of the time, possible members were unaware that they were being vetted for membership. A member suggested to Theo that a certain lady might fit in, and she then made her own inquiries about their suitability. Some were dismissed for not being convivial. She allowed no snide comments to upset her members, others for being blabbermouths who would risk their secrecy, and a few had taken being fast to extremes that went beyond what Theo considered acceptable. She still recalled the words from Perdita, which had snagged her heart, and convinced Theo to admit her despite her dubious background.

"I hunger to be free from the constraints of my life. Am I so selfish to desire to walk in the park without someone hovering? Is it so wrong to want to stroll with my hair down and tossing madly in the wind?"

Theo had gripped her gloved hand and said, *"No, my dear, and I have a place where you can get a slice of the freedom for which your heart hungers."*

Expectations had burned brightly in Perdie's eyes. *"Please do not take Lady Millicent to task…but…she mentioned that you are the owner and patroness of a most exclusive ladies' club, and I had so dearly hoped you would allow me to join you."*

Theo had been moved by her earnestness and

the hint of unhappiness in her eyes. "*At my club, we are a tiny bit scandalous. We partake in daring but such delightful wagers. I teach our girls how to fight…how to defend themselves from unwanted advances, we read scandalously wicked books that men believe we are not equipped to handle, we discuss political tracts, and we even let our hair down.*"

Perdita had burst into tears while wearing a wide smile. Theo hadn't the heart to deny her membership and since then had granted special admittance to three more debutantes. As long as they did not compromise the club's location or details, their membership was more than welcomed.

"I…" Perdie began. She took a deep breath. And another. "I am to be married."

That Theo had not expected. The young lady was one of her youngest members at nineteen, and she was not about much in society. In truth, Theo had never encountered her at a society ball. The first time they had met was in the British Museum halls, the following occasion a few days later at a circulating library, and then in Hyde Park. Lady Perdie had been alone, save for her companion. Theo had thought it unusual that no footmen accompanied the ladies but had thought perhaps her family might not be so wealthy.

Except the girl's dress had every appearance of fine quality with no expense spared. Theo hadn't probed, for she was also intimately familiar with the lengths a family would go to maintain the appearance they have when they are flushed with funds and were indeed broke and close to bankruptcy. Once, Theo's mother had chosen to buy a new ball gown for her daughter over purchasing coal for the winter.

"You do not seem overjoyed," Theo murmured.

"I…I *do* love him."

"I sense a but coming."

"I love Owen but…but I do not believe I am ready for marriage, Theo. He does not seem inclined to wait, and all he speaks about is our wedding which is to be held in Berkshire in eleven weeks and three days."

"I suspect you've been engaged long?"

At Perdie's look of inquiry, Theo said, "I've heard of no recent announcement on the marriage mart, and I am familiar with the matches made last season."

The girl sighed gustily. "I've known Lord Owen since I was fifteen. I swore I fell giddy in love with him at first sight. And he offered for my hand at seventeen. I thought it so romantic he said he wanted to capture my heart before I debuted on the marriage mart, for he did not want to lose me. My mother was happy with the match, and even my brother…who I believe is awfully hard to appease, seemed pleased. My brother did encourage me to have a season before I spoke of marriage matters, but I was so utterly determined to marry the man I love. I fear I was a little silly to decide on marriage so young. My brother approved the match after I agree to a two-year engagement."

Theo did not like that Perdie's tone lacked any sort of excitement. There only lingered the sharpest edge of frustration and disappointment. "How were your expectations dashed?"

The girl's throat worked on a swallow. "I…I did not need to join the other debutantes on the marriage mart because I had been lucky in love. I did not need a season, and I was quite content with that."

Perdie stood and started to pace. "I only traveled to London with mama to be fitted for my wedding trousseau. I've attended a few balls, I've been to the theater, I've been to museums, boat rides on the Thames…and inexplicably I woke one morning feeling as if…as if I've not lived, but I am getting married. Unexpectedly the walls felt closer, and I could not breathe. I felt…trapped!"

Her voice broke, and she pressed her face into her palms. "Oh, Theo, I've been feeling so wretched! I want to do much more before I have children of my own."

One of the maids arrived with a tea trolley. Theo waved her away and poured a steaming cup for Perdie. "Have you told this to your fiancé?"

Perdie made a sound of abject frustration. "I cannot have a decent conversation with him! All he speaks of is his love and how eager he is to start a family." A frown split her brows, and she said softly, "I do not want to be a mother so soon after marriage. I would like a long honeymoon and perhaps the chance to enjoy a few more seasons or even travel abroad. We are both young. I am nineteen, and he is one and twenty. I believed he would agree with my reasoning, but he is most opposed to the notion. Nothing I say seems to discourage him from pursuing such aims."

Perdie burst into tears, and Theo hurried to her side and gathered her into her arms. She stayed like that, holding the young girl to her side for several moments.

"Being here has been so wonderful," she hiccupped. "I…I do not wish to return to the country and marry. At least not yet. And I fear so deeply that he will not want to wait for me. I do not know what to do."

Theo rubbed the girl's shoulders. "You should speak to him frankly about the fears in your heart. I know as ladies, we are not encouraged to be direct with our opinions. However, marriage is not a simple matter. It is lifelong, Perdie. It is until death parts you. If you cannot be forthright with your husband, what is the point of it all?"

The girl nodded and appeared a bit calmer. She took a sip of her tea, appearing thoughtful. "And what if he does not listen?"

"From what you said, I gather that your brother dotes on you."

She bit into her lower lip. "Within reason. He… he is more like a father to me."

"He is much older than you then?"

"Yes, very much so."

"Is he uncompromising in his manner?"

The young girl groaned. "He can be, oh Theo, I do not think my brother will agree with me breaking the attachment. The scandal would…it would be horrific, and mama would not forgive me."

Theo suspected then Perdie's family might not be so influential in the *ton*, or surely her brother would be able to smooth things over with Lord Owen's family. Though it would be in his right to sue for breach of promise, the wider society did not seem aware of the engagement. Surely, with some persuasion, they might be able to come to a beneficial agreement.

"Is that what you want? To break the engagement?"

Fresh tears sprang to Perdie's eyes. "I do not know. He makes my heart beat so…and I swear I dream of him all the time! On our wedding day… of our family. But I also want to be like you!"

Theo jerked. "Like me?"

Wide eyes pinned her with fierce earnestness. "*Yes*. You are so incredibly beautiful and so free. When you laugh, you do so with your entire body, uncaring about what anyone thinks. You have this wonderful club that is the most *perfect* haven. I have

never felt as true to myself as I am when I am
under this roof. You attend the best balls, theatres;
I've seen you ride astride in the park! You are
clearly wealthy and a woman of style and fashion!
And surely you cannot be a day over thirty."

"I am only six and twenty," Theo said drily.
With a smile, she took Perdie's hand between hers.
"Perdie…I cannot tell you what to do if that is what
you are hoping. It might seem that I am free, and I
do suppose I am in many regards. But you seem to
have something that I have never truly known."

A skeptical frown split her brows. "I doubt
that."

"I have never known the love that you speak
about. A gentleman has never inspired my heart to
race or made me dream of him in the nights," she
replied candidly.

Perdie gasped. "Never?"

"Never."

"But you are a widow."

"My husband was a kind man, and there is love
in kindness, but not the kind of love that you feel. I
also have no…" Theo's throat closed, and for a
moment, a tight band hugged across her chest. The
viscount had made no attempt to be intimate with
her, informing her with little candor that his heavy
drinking had a great influence on his manhood and
passions. Theo had been relieved at the time until
she had understood it meant a life without children
or comfort or intimacy.

"I have no children, and I do not know if I ever shall. Perhaps one day, I might meet a gentleman who will understand my desire to own and operate a lady's club and one who might not mind the threat that hangs over our reputation for me owning it. *Perhaps*. My dearest friend, Prue, suggested it might be easier to find such a fabled dragon. You must carefully think of the things you are willing to give up and decide if you can bear to stand that cost."

A sob hitched in the girl's throat. "I do feel *terribly* confused. My heart pains me, like a physical ailment when I think about not marrying Owen. But when I think about marrying and starting a family, it is as if someone had placed a pillow over my face and pressed down."

Theo's heart squeezed, and the memory of feeling a similar agony when circumstances had forced her to marry a man thrice her age. She had been so young and naïve, believing only a grand love would take her to the wedding altar. How desperate she had been for another solution or for a listening ear.

"First, you must speak to your mother and your brother. Let them know your feelings on this matter and see what support you have from them. Do not be hasty to end the attachment. Love matches are rare. But you also need time, and I do believe it is important that your young man understands and values your feelings."

She flung herself into Theo's arms and hugged her. "Thank you, Theo!"

With a laugh, she returned her hug. "I am here anytime you wish to speak." And this moment reminded her why she had worked so hard to open this club, despite all the odds against its success. They drank a few cups of tea and chatted for almost an hour before Perdie departed. Her air of despondency had not vanished in its entirety, but there had been a marked improvement in her composure.

And that was all Theo could ask for at the moment.

A few hours later…

THEO LIFTED her head from the novel she'd been reading at the gentle clearing of a throat. The sheepish expression on her butler's face implied he'd tried capturing her attention a few times. An air of anxiety hovered about him that was quite unusual, for her butler was a man of experience in dealing with the many tomfooleries he'd witnessed under this roof. "Yes, Dobbs?"

"His Grace, the Duke of Hartford demands an audience, my lady."

Shocked seized Theo's throat for several seconds. She lowered the glass of sherry to the small table with a *clink* before putting away the book. "His Grace?"

"Yes, my lady."

She felt almost bereft of good senses at this precise moment. "The Duke of Hartford?"

"Yes, my lady."

Plucking the card from her butler's outstretched hand, she stared at it. *Good heavens.* What was he doing here? Not one person outside of the exclusive lady society had ever called at this address. The duke's presence even in the ballrooms cast a formidable shadow, so Theo understood her butler's ruffled nature. She had never personally met the man, but Theo had certainly heard of him.

What do I know of him?

She'd never crossed his path at any of the social events she attended over the last couple of years. Some rumors adroitly mentioned his lack of interest in the season's amusements and the marriage mart, given his long-standing connection with a certain family. It was expected by everyone the duke would eventually marry the Marquess of Bamforth's daughter. Lady Edith, herself, walked about with the airs and arrogance of a future duchess.

I do not know enough to come out ahead in any meeting with this man.

"Did he ask for me by name?"

"No, my lady. The duke demanded to see the master of the house. I…I did not feel I *could* disobey."

Oh, dear. "We cannot let His Grace inside."

"It is raining, my lady."

Theo briefly slammed her eyes closed. "Botheration! Inform the duke that I am not at home to callers, and I will call upon him at his earliest convenience."

His craggy features shifted into another expression and frowned, and her usually unflappable butler tugged at his necktie. "I truly do not believe the duke will accept that answer, my lady. There is something about him that was most...*compelling.*"

"Is that admiration I hear, Mr. Dobbs?"

His brows lowered even further at the coolness in her tone.

"The duke will not leave until he has seen the master of this home."

If not for Mr. Dobbs's advance years and his exemplary service in dealing with their shenanigans, Theo would have fired him just now. A *good* butler knew how to deflect unwanted callers, even if they were dukes. "Did you admit His Grace to the yellow parlor?"

Mr. Dobbs looked decidedly uncomfortable, and she frowned. To Theo's mind, there was no other room in the lavish townhouse suited to receive a gentleman caller. In truth, her home was no ordinary townhouse fitted to receive any eligible callers of society. Theo acknowledged then she had not prepared adequately for this moment, and she had known it was possible someone unexpected could arrive one day. "Well?"

"Lady Hatfield and Miss Lavinia are still in the yellow parlor discussing the chapter they had just read together of *Robinson Crusoe*."

That novel had made it onto their book club list because one of their members', Lady Sylvia's, guardian had banned her from reading it, with the inane reasoning that it might induce hysterics given her delicate nerves. It would not do to disturb their rousing debates of its themes. Nor would Theo know where to put them, with most of the rooms being occupied. His Grace being on her doorstep felt like a disaster. How clever she had thought herself to be having their ladies club in plain sight.

"Then where is the duke?"

"He…he is still on the doorstep, my lady," her butler said, clearly distressed. "We've never had a gentleman caller before, and all other parlors are occupied."

"You left a *duke* on the doorstep?"

"Yes, my lady."

"And in the rain?"

"That is why I mentioned it was raining, my lady."

"Good heavens!" Theo knew of Hartford's rumored power and influence. The duke was not a man to be left on anyone's doorstep, in the rain no less! Theo hurried to her feet, skirted around Mr. Dobbs, and rushed through the open door of her private parlor out into the long hallway to skid to an alarming halt.

A tall, powerfully built gentleman stood in the hallway, removing his hat, and glancing around with an expression of chilling insouciance. If this was the duke, the man had invited himself inside. She must have made a sound, for his head snapped around before he faltered into stillness.

Theo's breath caught in her chest at the rugged handsomeness of the man in her hallway. His dark hair appeared windswept and in desperate need of a trim. His mouth was a tight, determined line, and he radiated certainty and purpose. He shrugged from a coat, sprinkling water droplets onto the floor. Her butler hurried past her to collect the man's hat, jacket, and a walking cane.

The duke was impeccably dressed in tan breeches, a white shirt with a burgundy waistcoat, and jacket. Shockingly he wore no cravat, and his knee-high boots suggested he'd been out riding. Even with the distance between them, the blue of his eyes was stunningly discernable. *And what a magnificent blue they were*. Those eyes pinned her with a hawkish and very rude stare as they ran over her with thorough insolence.

Theo sensed his curiosity in the same manner she could sense her heartbeat in her throat. *Was this…was this the duke?* Or had someone else dared to invade her home without an express invitation? Nerves leaped inside Theo's body, and she smoothed her dark yellow day gown, conscious of the cool tiles beneath her feet.

The duke's eyes missed nothing, lingering in places a gentleman of good conduct had no place looking. His accusatory gaze lingered on her feet bare of stockings and shoes! He stared at her toes, and she reflexively curled them on the cool mosaic tiles. Theo almost blushed but instead lifted her chin, hoping to portray a cool composure. Still, a peculiar warmth hooked low in her belly and tugged.

Good heavens, what is this nonsense?

CHAPTER THREE

*I*t is just an unexpected reaction to how handsome he is, she silently said, *gather yourself and greet him.* Before she could speak, his voice snapped out a cold, crisp command.

"I will see the master of this house at once."

It would be ill-mannered in the extreme to try and turn him away, though she was very tempted to at least try. Theo's chest lifted on a ragged breath. That soft sound tugged his gaze to her face, and she could see that he had drawn a very unflattering supposition. Squaring her shoulders and lifting her chin, Theo took a few steps toward him before pausing at a respectable distance. "You are the Duke of Hartford."

His nostrils flared as the man looked down his perfect nose at her for possibly daring to not know him.

"I am."

"Your Grace, may I invite you to the drawing-room?"

"And you are?"

How chillingly arrogant he sounded. Theo dipped into a quick but elegant curtsy. "Lady Theodosia Winfern, Your Grace."

His gaze sharpened. "Relative to the late Viscount Winfern?"

"I am his widow."

The duke's gaze swept over her once again, and she prevented herself from curling her toes.

"I gather you are the mistress here."

"I am, Your Grace."

The duke's expression shuttered. "I see."

His hardened jaw gave no clue as to his thoughts.

Theo offered him a polite smile. "And exactly what do you see, Your Grace?"

A pregnant pause filled the silence, and the curiosity in his regard deepened. "If you will lead the way, Lady Winfern, this is a conversation best held in privacy."

She tried not to show any reaction to his words. Theo turned around and walked back toward the private drawing-room that she had commanded as her own. Laughter spilled from the winding staircase, and Theo winced as Lady Humphrey, and Miss Louisa Charlton appeared on the steps. A loud gasp sounded, drawing the duke's stare and his steps faltered.

"Your Grace!" Countess Humphrey cried, blushing.

She threw Theo a shocked, scandalized look, and she understood why. They both had bare feet, with their gorgeous hair unpinned and rippling down their shoulders. The nature of their déshabillé was suspicious and scandalous, even if they were indoors.

"Lady Humphrey," he said with indifferent civility, his eyes taking in every detail. "I had not expected to see you here."

What had he expected? The countess appeared too stunned to form a reply. Theo smiled upon her patrons reassuringly, hating that they seemed so startled and out of sorts. This was supposed to be a haven, a place where they could relax and be themselves without any fear of censure, and she had thoughtlessly allowed someone to intrude.

Duke or not, Theo should have managed the unexpected encounter better. An unwanted sensation lodged inside her chest. "His Grace called unexpectedly to discuss a business matter perhaps. Please, do not mind his presence. He will be leaving shortly, and his discretion is very much assured."

How she would achieve that she had no idea as yet, but she could not allow His Grace to leave without receiving his word of honor to keep silent. Theo would have to be very delicate in how she extracted that promise. He must give it without understating that he was protecting the location of a clandestine club for ladies of the *ton*.

She sashayed toward the door she'd left ajar, acutely aware of his probing gaze on her back. Theo preceded the duke inside and made her way over to a large wing back chair and sat. The duke's gaze swept the room, a small frown spilling his brows. Fading sunlight shone through the large sash windows, and a fireplace burned low in the hearth. The drawing-room was spacious, and the folding doors leading to the ballroom were open. Thankfully, it was empty. Earlier, there had been dancing lessons for ladies who believed themselves awkward and possessed of two left feet. Here, they learned to dance at their pace, without any shoes pinching their feet, their hair let down, and with the condemning eyes of the *ton* absent.

Theo waved a hand to the sofa closest to her. "If you would like to sit, Your Grace, I invite you to do so. I am quite keen to hear why you've unexpectedly paid a call to my home."

The duke did not appear to hear her. His entire attention was commanded elsewhere, and she bit back a groan to see that he stared at the large wagering board taking up half of the south wall. Her heart jolted. Good heavens, the duke's name was on the board. Theo hurriedly stood. "Your Grace!" she said sharply.

There was another board to the left which outlined a betting guide for those who might wish to wager on any of the happenings of high society. The board he stared at listed the current wagers, some naughtier than the others. There were several open wagers and a few dares.

1. *Will the Duke of Hartford marry Lady Edith by season's end?* Certainly, harmless to Theo's way of thinking.
2. *Will Lady Peabody bear her husband a son or daughter?* Another harmless wager.
3. *A pot of one hundred pounds is to be had for the lady who dared to steal back a certain packet of love letters from Lord Sallis.* A bit wickeder, but still, none of the duke's business. Nor would she explain a dare was very much different from a wager, and they dared each other often to act with wonderful impetuosity and a bit of wicked recklessness.
4. *Viscount Thurgood famously declared the next lady to drop her handkerchief in front of him will find herself thoroughly kissed. Who here will take on this dare?* At least five names had been scandalously written beside that one.

The duke faced Theo, and she was struck by the piercing blue of his eyes and how they fell on her. It was as if he dissected her, assessing each part. "How outrageous and daring you are," he said with icy incivility, his eyes unflinching on her person.

Theo stepped even closer and just as softly, replied, "You intruded quite unexpectedly, Your Grace. If I had known you would call, I would have removed your name."

His icy gaze felt like it burned her insides. "What is this place?"

Upon her husband's death four years ago, she'd found herself with more than enough wealth to create her very own secret ladies' club, very much in the manner of those popular gentleman clubs— White's and Brooks, but with more elegance. Their members simply referred to their place of haven as 48 Berkeley Square.

All her clients were respectable ladies of society who felt confined by their family and the ton's duties and expectations. Once upon a time, Theo had been one of those ladies, one who had been forced by her family to marry a man three times her age. A man with a reputation of being a libertine who liked to gamble. But he had been a viscount, one with a lot of money which her family needed.

Theo had created this club for ladies who were told they had only one purpose in this life: to be whatever their family and society decided. And that was to place all their hopes and dreams in a pretty box and lock it away. They should exist for their family's needs and not their own. How dare they have desires and hopes for themselves. 48 Berkeley

Square was a sanctuary of sorts. In this place, a lady could sneak off to relax, have more than one glass of claret, smoke a cheroot, remove their hair from the severe style arrangements, walk barefoot, and take part in wicked wagers and oftentimes harebrained dares. What was most important was they had fun, and every lady loved being here. This damned duke had no right to question that.

How dare he presume to judge her life, and in that insolent, condescending manner? "This is my home, Your Grace."

"I will not ask again, Lady Winfern, and it is best you do not test my patience."

Theo glared at him, not liking the shaky feeling winding its way through her heart. "What right do you have to demand anything of me, Your Grace? You are the interloper uninvited and trespassing in *my home*. I implore you to state your business."

It was clear the man was not used to anyone speaking back to him in such a bold and unconcerned manner. Theo drew on all the teachings she'd learned over the years to present a serene composure. Inside she was quaking and resented that he could stir such alarm within her.

"Your home," he repeated flatly.

"Yes."

"Where you gamble on matters not concerning yourself?" he asked with chilling incivility.

"How hypocritical," she drawled.

"Tread carefully, Lady Winfern."

"Or what? You might bite?" Theo snapped provocatively.

He was so much taken aback for a moment he said nothing. Then his gaze narrowed on her, and he softly replied, "Yes, and I have large, powerful teeth."

Theo returned his regard, trying to take a measure of the man. "I have it on the highest authority a bet placed at White's only a few days ago was on who Lady Sophia Fairfax might choose as her suitor! Another speculation with an exceptionally large purse is on who the widowed Lady Twickenham will take as her protector. Is it Marquess Argyle or the more dashing Earl Raymore?"

"You compare your outrageous boards to the wagers set at White's?" he demanded with an arched brow. "It is a gentleman's club. Wagers are a bedrock of their activities."

She smiled. "And at my home, my guests can do whatever they wish."

"Guests like the countess."

Of course, he hadn't forgotten the countess's state of déshabillé.

"It is of no concern of yours, Your Grace," Theo said mildly, "Who I have as guests and what they do here. Now, how might I help you this afternoon."

"How unflappable you are," he drawled with a small curve to his mouth.

Theo almost gasped, for she felt that small smile way down in her belly, an unanticipated curl of heat that blossomed outward and set her heart to racing. *How utterly absurd!*

"I do beg your pardon, is there something I should be afraid of?" Without waiting for his reply but very conscious of his scrutiny upon her body, Theo walked to the mantle and poured brandy into two glasses. Padding over to him, she offered him one of the glasses, which he took. His gaze was shrewd, and she detected the cunning brilliance in his eyes. The duke evidently assessed what he knew so far, and though Theo thought it was extraordinarily little, there was knowledge in his eyes.

"The countess just now was very shocked to see me in this domain. The young miss beside her looked ready to faint. Walking down the hallway just now, the small glimpse into the rooms with open doors show a décor of feminine grace and beauty. There is no touch indicating a man lives here or that there are any expectations of any gentleman callers. That is why the countess appeared so shocked." He walked over to the board, his expression inscrutable. "And you have a wagering board…very much like the wager books we have at White's and Brooks. The winner of the wager will receive the sum noted here."

"How astute," she said quite blandly.

He took a healthy swallow of the brandy. "Your

home is a meeting place for ladies of the *ton*. A salon of sorts…a club perhaps?"

Her composure, so laboriously acquired, trembled. How little effort it took to achieve his conclusion. "Whatever my home is, of what concern is it yours?" Theo asked, lifting her glass to her lip, and taking a demur sip impervious to his outraged scrutiny.

The duke studied her with an air of befuddlement. "Any sort of club is a gentleman's domain for a reason, Lady Winfern."

"Surely you agree there are some things that *cannot* be exclusive to men." Theo smiled. "Wagers are an amusing pastime that cannot only be owned by your sex. At least we ladies are sensible in our gambling. Only a mean-spirited beast would dare to censure us."

"A mean-spirited beast, am I?"

"Oh dear, never say you *are* censuring us. Such hypocrisy when your most famous wager was about two raindrops falling down the pane of glass in a particular bow window," she said with biting sarcasm. "How *pre-historic* you are. I cannot fathom why society wonders at your unmarried state."

He stared at her as if she were the rarest creature plucked from thin air and dropped in front of him. To Theo's surprise, his mouth twitched, and amusement darkened his cobalt eyes. Unexpectedly she was assailed by an odd sort of awareness.

"You do not want to make an enemy of me, Lady Theodosia," he murmured.

The silence stretched out, broken only by the faint chime of the drawing-room clock.

"I cannot contrive how I would accomplish *that*. Surely you mistake the matter that has you so out of sorts."

"Is Lady Perdita a patron of your establishment?"

Theo's heart jolted. Perdie had not owned to being intimately acquainted with a duke! Especially one as formidable as Hartford. "Forgive me, Your Grace, I must maintain the strictest of confidence the identity of the ladies who visit my home, I am sure you understand."

"I came here expecting to find a bounder," he said. "A Gentleman who had taken ruthless advantage of my sister, one who encouraged her to lie to her family and act in a most secretive manner."

His sister? Theo's thoughts raced. "Your Grace, no gentleman is living on this premises, nor do I accept male visitors. You…you are a first. That is the reason you so flustered my butler he left you on the doorstep."

He took a long swallow of his brandy before replying, "My sister has been lying and visiting here for over a month. She has lied to me, her mother, and her fiancé. If your club is above scrutiny, I wonder at the deception."

Theo clasped her hands before her. Many of the ladies who joined their close society did not reveal to their families the true nature of their indulgences here. Theo understood. "Given the nature of our… activities and the harsh and oftentimes ridiculous expectations society can have of us ladies, I…I suspect Lady Perdie believes you might not approve."

And each member had vowed to uphold their society's confidence unless they believed someone else might also need the haven.

"And this is the kind of behavior your society encourages and condones?" he asked bitingly, not removing his gaze from the wagering board.

Theo almost snapped and asked what fascinated him so about the wagers. Though she admitted a few were scandalous, most were just fun and harmless. "Your Grace, Lady Perdie would have only joined because she felt something is missing in her life," Theo said softly. "Our members are few, but we are remarkably close-knit, and the common bond that usually draws us together is that we are not fully happy with the life we are living. Here is just a place to have deeper friendship and be true to our hearts."

"Young ladies lie and manipulate their families to be a part of your exclusivity." He faced her, and the cold accusation in his eyes stung. "I suppose you charge them a fee as well."

He spoke with such quelling hauteur, Theo

flushed. "You mistake the matter; I've never asked anyone to directly lie, Your Grace."

"Ah…I now understand the distinction you use to justify lies and deception. I've never heard about this club of yours, not even a hint in the scandal sheets. How do you suppose your members retain this anonymity you must have demanded?"

The air between them crackled with challenge.

"Secrecy is a part of our membership, and only by referral can someone join us. But I have never asked anyone to lie. They can tell their families or husband they are calling at my home."

His expression remained inscrutable as he considered her, and Theo got the awful feeling this man might consider her the enemy. The very notion of it was frightening, for he had the power to ruin her. It was one of the reasons she'd kept her lady's society a secret, for the very idea of it would offend those who thought themselves morally superior, but hypocritically behind closed doors had offensive conduct the women in their lives disparaged. Then some would loathe the idea of ladies simply existing in a space that did not uphold their ridiculous expectations of what they deemed lady-like conduct.

"You must have been happy to land the sister of a duke in your cap. Take your ambitions elsewhere," he ordered.

She tried to ignore the thumping of her heart. "I had no notion Perdie was the relative of a duke. I have no ambitions concerning our friendship, Your Grace!"

Those dissecting eyes settled on her once more; this time the silence was thoughtful. Finally, he replied, "Her association with…with your home ends today. You will terminate Lady Perdie's membership effectively."

Theo gasped. "Your Grace, surely now that you know what happens here, it is permissible for Perdie—"

"It is not."

A surge of frustration went through Theo's heart. She hadn't thought the duke a sanctimonious prude! The memory of how unhappy Perdie had been in those first days rose in Theo's thoughts. Perdie had been forlorn but had not spoken about what troubled her thoughts. The young girl had eventually relaxed her guard and revealed a warm and carefree soul with an aptitude for fencing and Greek. Earlier she had seemed so relieved to have unburdened her cares. It showed she had no one at home to confide her fears, hopes, and expectations.

"Your Grace," Theo said, keeping her tone warm and moderate, hoping to reach a clearly hardened heart. "I carefully guide the ladies who are members of my club without being overly restrictive. *Nothing* we do here is wicked or wanton or disgraceful. We partake in wagers, but as you can see, they *are* harmless. We have a reading club. A fencing and boxing club, more for exercise than anything else."

He did not need to know it was a bit more vigorous than that and aimed at teaching ladies how to defend their virtues from lecherous and persistent rakes! "Above all, what we have here is *genuine* friendship. I believe it will hurt Lady Perdie to terminate her membership. She finds a friendship she can trust in me, and I find in her a younger sister and a friend. Please, if you will reconsider that she joined for a reason before you act in haste."

"I expect the termination to happen by tomorrow."

She wanted to smack him for his obstinacy. "Or else?"

The duke seemed entirely arrested by that challenge. The way he stared at her...Theo curled her toes into the thick carpet.

"I will dismantle your little club brick by brick until there is nothing left," he said with ruthless assurance.

Theo stared at him, her heart pounding, for he had the power and connections to crumple everything she worked for with little effort. "Am I so ineligible to be a friend of your sister?"

"Yes."

She contained her affronted gasp, hating to admit that she felt the pain of his rejection in her heart. Utter rubbish for she did not know this man!

"Then you inform your sister yourself that she may not visit me anymore."

"I have already spoken," he said, and turned away.

The man was leaving.

"You are using me to do your dirty work," she said, anger snapping through her veins. "To prohibit Perdie from coming here ever again will hurt her terribly. Of course, you will force me to do it for you, so she will not be angry or disappointed with you, but very much so with me for callously dashing her hopes and trampling on the joy she found here."

The duke faced her, his eyes flashing a cool warning. "You invited a young lady here without doing your due diligence under whose protection and care she fell. No doubt you only cared about lining your pocket with your fees and making social-climbing connections."

Theo's gasp of sheer outrage strangled in her throat.

"I was not considered in the formation of this agreement…and I do not need to be there when it is broken. I bid you a good day, Lady Winfern."

"Your Grace!" Theo took a few bracing breaths. "I…I must secure your word of honor that you will not mention what you have seen here today."

"And do I have your word of honor that my sister will no longer be allowed here?"

Theo understood this negotiation, and she

my return. Once I have your agreement, my discretion in this matter is very much assured. Do we understand each other?"

The lady's golden-brown eyes flashed with anger, and her delicate toes curled into the carpet. He mildly wondered if she imagined lifting her feet and kicking him. Somehow that notion did not surprise him. She had pretty feet too. There was a quiet, fine-boned quality to her features that might give one the impression Lady Winfern was delicate. To Seb's mind, nothing could be further from the truth. The lady was a spitfire. His impression of the woman before him was quiet strength, boldness, and impetuosity. A most dangerous combination in his experience. She would keep any man on his toes.

"I understand, Your Grace," she said after a few tense moments. "I will speak with Lady Perdie."

He saw it had cost her to make the admission and that her pride had suffered a blow. Sebastian wasn't here to pander to her feelings but to save his sister's dignity and reputation. And to also protect her heart. "Do not make me your enemy," he said, assessing the determined lift to that stubborn chin. "You will surely regret it."

Somewhere during the eleven years he had acted as a father to Perdie, he must have failed her or let her down abominably for her to believe she had to lie to him to visit here. All that deception would end now. Without awaiting Lady Winfern's reply, he turned away and made it down the long hallway. Sebastian collected his top hat and coat from the butler, putting them on before exiting the townhouse. Walking down the cobbled steps into the still trickling rain, he slowed his steps. Two ladies with their hands looped together, and heads bent close were walking toward the townhouse. They froze upon seeing him, their pretty expressions were of comical dismay. Sebastian tipped his hat and made his way past them and to his parked carriage waiting a few houses down. He would not disclose to any but his mother what he found here. There was hardly much scandalous about it since even his mother hosted her monthly salon with notable society ladies. Though he suspected Lady Winfern and her band of ladies got up to more mischief than book discussion.

That damn wager board had his name on it. Everyone in society seemed to be betting on Lady Edith becoming his duchess. How ridiculous they all were.

A ladies' club.

Nothing much had the power to surprise Sebastian anymore. But this did. She did. Her long eyelashes, flowing golden-brown hair, full breasts, inviting curves, and lips made to tempt the heavens.

Heat rushed to his groin, and his heartbeat thundered in his ears.

Nothing much had the power to entice his senses, but Lady Theodosia Winfern most astonishingly did with little effort on her part. His first sight of her had struck him into stillness.

She was truly ravishing.

The lady was also a rebellious spitfire who had encouraged his sister to be deceptive with her family. And she did not seem afraid of his power but truly possessed the audacity to challenge him. This he had not expected when he arrived on her doorstep, expecting to issue a duel to the bounder who dared to seduce his sister.

What do I know of you?

Though he'd accused her of being callous in charging a fee to her members, Lady Winfern should be a wealthy woman because of her late husband. Though a renowned gambler, the man had not been broke, and Sebastian had had several business dealings with the late viscount. His widow's reputation was a bit absurd, for she had married a man thrice her age. It had clearly been for his money and title, and people in the *ton* frowned on such obviously vulgar reasons for marrying. Sebastian found their hypocrisy pitiful. Everyone in the *ton* married for power and connections. They were simply cunning and very discreet about it. Love matches were a rare delight that was often met with sly whispers. With her beauty and lack of fortune, the lady had simply been obviously unrefined with her choice, and they'd had a grand time cutting her down for it.

There was a betting book at White's overflowing

with wagers over who would eventually win the lady's hand. Not for marriage, but to be their mistress. Her experience with the world and the lifestyle she lived was not for his young, willful sister. Especially when it had turned her into a creature who would lie so easily to her family, and one who would treat the young man who loved her with such dismissive contempt.

Upon reaching his carriage, he rattled off instructions to take him to his club. Hauling himself inside, he settled against the squabs, almost annoyed with himself to still have the sensual image of Lady Winfern lingering in his thoughts. Beyond this encounter, the lady had no reason to stay within his thoughts. It was unlikely he would see her again or have reason to converse with her. Sebastian was a man of his words. He would tell no one of her salon.

The carriage drew to a stop in St. James's Street, and he alighted and strolled toward White's. He entered, returning greetings from the gentlemen sitting around smoking and drinking brandy. Sebastian entered the dining room, anticipating the delight to his palette. The chef was truly inspired, rumor saying he had been stolen from the king's kitchens.

Once seated, a freshly pressed newspaper, a decanter of brandy together with a glass was promptly delivered. A shadow fell over him, and he glanced up to spy Percy Deveraux, Marquess of Wolverton, and Sebastian's closest friend.

"I haven't seen you here in days," Percy said, inviting himself to sit. "I thought you busy with estate matters in Sussex."

Lowering the newspaper, Sebastian replied, "A letter to my steward was the only thing needed. I decided it's best to remain in town while Perdie is here."

"Ah, how is the little imp doing?"

"Not so little anymore, but still as willful."

Percy grunted and tugged at his cravat. "Reminds me of someone who is a thorn in my side," he said darkly. "Do you know I caught the chit *climbing* from her bedroom window? Nearly gave me apoplexy."

The man spoke of a young lady, Miss Frederica Williams, who had become his ward these past two years. The young lady would be about Perdie's age, and she resented every inch of the restrictions befitting the station Percy had tried to foist on her. His friend seemed increasingly frustrated with Miss Williams, but Sebastian did not think his friend was aware that the more he spoke of the lady, a throb of longing entered his tone. Percy was beginning to see her as a woman, and Seb suspected this young lady was the reason his friend had cut all connection with his mistress several months previous.

"It is as if there is something in the air encouraging

the ladies of society to rebellion. Did you know Thomas's once biddable sister, whom he found a most excellent match, suddenly ordered a new wardrobe, cut her hair, and informed him she will find her own husband? Thomas has no idea what to do with Lady Charity. It must be something in the damn air."

Or that something is Lady Theodosia Winfern.

"Why has that amused you?" Percy demanded archly, filling his glass with whisky.

"It was but a thought about a lady."

Percy leered. "Ah, are you procuring a mistress at last? It is about time!"

Sebastian ignored that dig and the punch low in his gut at the thought of having that particular lady in his bed, and his cock buried deep. His carnal imagination told him she would be a most passionate lover, giving and receiving in equal measure. "I am about to select my duchess. The last thing I am thinking about is a mistress or a lover."

"Bloody hell," his friend said with a mock shudder. "Never say you are really putting on the old ball and chain."

Seb grinned. "You'll marry eventually. It is stupid to dread something natural and inevitable. What you need to do is be smart about it. Make a list of the eligible ladies and select a lady for your wife."

"That sounds damnable cold-blooded. Selecting a wife on paper."

"With the number of ladies out in society, do

you have another way? I assure you, these ladies and their mothers do the same when considering a husband. They weigh his title, his yearly income, and his connections. A list is formed, and then the hunt starts with whoever is at number one. Never say you were ignorant of such matters," he said with a mocking lift of his glass.

His friend scowled and adroitly changed the subject. Seb relaxed into his chair, shifting the conversation into politics seamlessly. Surprisingly as they chatted about the bills that had been voted down in the last parliament session, the lush image of Viscountess Winfern lingered in his thoughts as if she had been permanently interred there.

.

CHAPTER FIVE

One week later…

*P*erdie appeared resplendent in a high-waisted peach gown, a golden sash tied around her waist, silken gloves hugged her slim arms, and her hair had been fashioned in a riot of curls atop her head. She danced the waltz with Lord Owen, and while he smiled at her, wearing his love on his sleeves, her smiles were dimmed.

That affected Sebastian. His sister did not seem happy, and it gutted him something fiercely. This morning when they broke their fast as a family, he tried to get her to open up in a conversation, but she had been very tightlipped. The opposite of her usual garrulous nature. Even his mother was concerned, but Perdie had assured them all it was the excitement and plans for her wedding which made her seem so wan.

The tight band across his chest eased when she laughed at something Lord Owen said. Seb could not hear that lovely chortle, but from where he stood on the balcony's upper story, he clearly saw the radiance of her smile.

His shoulders relaxed, and for the first time since that evening, he was able to take his attention from her and direct it toward another lady. Lady Edith held court with her coterie on the sidelines, her fan unfurled, and the lady sweeping it gently back and forth. She hadn't danced for the evening, and not for lack of being asked. A few times she stared directly at him, and Sebastian sensed she waited for him to come and ask her. The seductive lure was there whenever her gaze caught his, yet he was not compelled to rush to her side and request her hand for the dancefloor.

It seemed the lady herself had decided he would be her husband. He felt nothing but mild amusement and perhaps a bit of admiration at Lady Edith's certainty. Seb did admire a lady who knew what she wanted and went for it because he owned similar traits. Lady Edith had made it to the very top of his list of candidates for his duchess, for the lady was exemplary in her reputation, connections, and qualities. And he recalled her being a lively conversationalist who hadn't believed her topics of discourse should be limited.

A flash of green caught Seb's attention, a mass of honey gold hair piled high, a string of pearls lovingly clasped around a most delicate throat. The lady's gown clung enticingly to her curves and revealed a delectable swell of her cleavage. She met with several ladies by a large potted plant, and he idly wondered if they were other members of her club.

The lady tipped back her head and laughed, arching the delicate line of her throat. *Bloody hell.* Theodosia Winfern imbued sensuality and such charm that something raw and unfathomable stirred low in Seb's gut. He imagined setting the tip of his tongue to her lush mouth, then going down to gently nibble the flesh of her throat, right where her pulse would be fluttering. He could taste the soft dewiness of her skin, hear the soft, breathless whimper she would make as he continued licking his way downward. Seb's heart pounded, and he found himself gripping the railing of the balustrade.

Perdie, who strolled in Lady Winfern's direction, stopped as if she'd slammed into a wall. Her face crumpled, and she whirled away, hurrying in the opposite direction. Lady Winfern evidently had upheld her end of the bargain. Though he had suspected her of having done so. For Perdie had not attempted to bribe the coachman to sneak her away in the past few days but had spent her time accepting callers with his mother, practicing her music on the grand pianoforte, and taking long strolls with Lord Owen.

Oddly, no satisfaction filled Seb. Confoundingly, it had much to do with the flash of a pained grimace on Lady Winfern's lovely face, that lingering shadow of hurt and loss. She stared after his sister with such aching regret, somewhere in the vicinity of his heart squeezed.

There had been a friendship there, and his command had hurt that bond, possibly broken it irrevocably because the once cheerful demeanor his sister bravely showed these last few days was also a façade. She was not happy, and once again, he had missed it. His sister said something to his mother, who held her own court by the ballroom's south side. Their mother nodded, and Perdie exited the ballroom.

What was going on?

Sebastian made his way down the staircase and through the crush to his sister. Once in the hallway, he spied her walking deeper into the household.

"Perdie," he said.

Despite the loud chatter and music, his sister whirled to face him, and a rush of worry went through him. There was a strain about her mouth as if she was hurt and was doing everything in her power not to crumble.

"Are you well?" he asked upon reaching her.

She rubbed at her temple. "I fear I have a megrim. Mamma suggested I call for the carriage and head home to bed, but I prefer to rest within the library or the parlor."

"Would you like my silent company?" Though he wished to converse with her, the strain around her mouth suggested the head pain was unpleasant.

"No, brother, believe me when I say some time alone is what I need. I might rejoin the party after an hour or so of rest. It is very early yet, and there is much more dancing to do."

He removed a small watch from his pocket and glanced at the time. It was merely ten p.m. "I will no longer withdraw to my club. I'll stay...perhaps even do a spot of dancing, and whenever you need me, send a servant for me."

Her eyes lit up. "You? Dancing? I will be saddened to miss such a spectacle."

"You are so convinced I am going to fumble?" he teased, chucking her slightly under her chin.

She wrinkled her nose. "I spoke of the *delightful* spectacle of everyone's reaction. I've heard more than one lady just tonight refer to you as a prime article, how much they would swoon to have a mere glance from you, *and* how very fortunate Lady Edith is to own your regard."

"You exaggerate, but it has reminded me it would be best if I withdraw to the card room."

"I did see Lord Wolverton escaping there earlier."

Seb escorted her to a small inviting parlor that had a fire lit in the hearth. Perdie walked away from him to seat herself on the sofa closest to the fire. A relieved sigh slipped from her when she eased back into the padded cushions. "Please let Mama know that I shall be fine resting here for a few hours."

"I will." Sebastian headed from the parlor only to pause at the whisper of his name. Turning to face Perdie, he replied, "Yes?"

She stared at him for a moment, an indecipherable look in her eyes. A rush of worry went through Sebastian. "Is all well, Perdie?"

"I love you," she said with a soft smile.

"I love you too, poppet." Then he opened the door and walked out into the hall, unsure why a heavy press of disquiet lingered in his heart.

THE BALL HOSTED by Lady Prudence Campbell, the Countess of Wycliffe, was a successful crush. Her face carried a happy glow, and Theo squeezed her hand reassuringly. "Your ball is perfectly splendid."

"I cannot believe so many people came," she breathed happily, her dark green eyes glittering with triumph. "My very first ball is a success. I am so very glad I accepted your dare, Theo, and you owe me fifty pounds which I will be donating to my beloved charity!"

Theo smiled. "I knew it would be splendid. You *are* the Countess Wycliffe. It is time the *ton* knows it, and that is best done with a lavish ball."

"It is also time for my lord to know I am his countess," Prue murmured, her gaze going to her imposing and very dashing husband who had recently entered the ballroom.

Since their marriage three years ago, Prue had spent most of her time in the country, except for this season when she had boldly stepped into town, shaking the barrier the earl seemed to place around their marriage and relationship.

"Since his entrance, he has not stopped staring at you," Theo said with a light laugh. "*That* is most glorious."

The man's eyes devoured his wife's voluptuous form like a hungry wolf, yet he did not approach her or ask for her hand in a dance. Everyone expected the earl and countess to take to the dancefloor once the waltz was announced, and Theo feared the blasted man would disappoint his wife's expectation and bruise her tender feelings. Their union hadn't been a love match, and the earl had made little effort to grow close to his countess. Theo faced Prue and gave her a reassuring smile. "Well done."

The countess's eyes swept the packed ballroom. "It seems Perdie has left already. She has ignored all my overtures."

A painful weight settled across Theo's chest. "I fear I hurt her dreadfully. I have not been able to sleep well since I told her she is no longer welcome at 48 Berkeley Street. I must find a way to fix it. I did explain it was only temporary, but I do not think she believed me."

Prue snapped her fan open with agile swiftness, the edge covering her mouth. "Upon my word, someone *very* eligible and a bit wicked this way comes."

The excited alarm in Prue's voice had Theo whirling around. Her heart lurched to see the Duke of Hartford, looking terribly handsome, cutting a swathe directly toward their location. Theo's heart beat erratically with curiosity and fascination as he came closer. She had seen him earlier up in the upper balcony but had not dreamed the man would approach her.

"I do believe he is coming to you, Theo," Prue said, the fan masking the rapid movement of her mouth. "And *everyone* is staring."

They most certainly were.

"Do you know the duke, Theo?"

"I…" *Botheration*. Her cheeks heated, and for a brief moment, she wondered if it might be wise to escape into the gardens. Perhaps it was better they met publicly. "He is the true reason I stopped Perdie from visiting us."

"Upon my word, you are entirely serious! You kept that from us," Prue said accusingly. "Why ever would you do so? That was a piece of most pertinent information, Theo."

She swallowed a rising groan. The club and all its happenings were her responsibility. Theo hadn't wanted to involve her dear friends with the intimate threat from the duke. They would have worried and tried to interfere. "The duke is Perdie's brother."

"I thought her brother an old, uncompromising man," Prue said, looking a bit troubled.

"She was very wide of the mark with that description though I can very well believe he is uncompromising in his manners. He paid an unexpected visit to 48 Berkeley Square about a week ago and demanded I end her membership. Since he warned me to stay clear of his path, I cannot fathom why he should approach me. Unless it is not me."

"Pish! It is you. His regard borders on scandalous!"

The duke was indeed too intense, uncaring that he stared at her in such an encompassing manner, uncaring that a few notable lords tried to capture his attention. Being the sole regard of this man's stare had an uncomfortable and very heated sensation fluttering low in her belly and embarrassingly even lower. Theo had never reacted so to any man, and she felt flustered.

"To my regret, I did what he demanded," Theo murmured. "I cannot imagine why he should approach me now."

Prue touched her hand. "You made the right decision."

"Did I? Lady Perdie is clearly unhappy, and I gave in without fighting for her. I have been so wretched since trying to find a solution. I thought perhaps I should pay her a call this week. We do not need to be friends only through the club."

"And will the duke agree?"

"Hang the duke," she said, vexation surging in her heart.

"The duke is not a man you want to cross."

No, he was a man she actually dreamed of kissing three nights in a row to her undying shame. Theo could not deceive herself; she was awfully attracted to the duke, enough so she found herself wondering what it would be like to dance within his arms, to perhaps press her mouth against his. The admission horrified her. He was a man uncaring of his sister's tender sensibilities and the hopes in her heart.

It has been a long time since a man inspired Theo to girlish fantasies of kissing and dancing. It quite irritated her the duke evoked these feelings inside without any indication that he might have felt a similar attraction. What woman would want to kiss that stern, arrogant mouth?

The orchestra of twenty souls leaped to life, and the opening strains of the waltz rode the air. Thrilled ladies and gentlemen moved into the wide-open space reserved for dancing.

"Lady Winfern," the duke greeted, bending into a quick bow.

He straightened, and his gaze pierced hers. His eyes truly were striking…magnificent, appearing even darker with an emotion she could not discern.

A long-suppressed sensation stirred in the pit of Theo's stomach and an ache of want settled low in her belly. The visceral feeling shocked her, and she dipped in a quick curtsey. "Your Grace, a pleasure to see you again."

A dangerous thing to admit even to oneself. Ladies like her and dukes were not friends. What was there to feel pleasure about when he had been beastly?

His eyes were cold and unpleasantly cynical. "Is it a pleasure?"

"Perhaps only mildly pleasant," replied Theo, with utmost candor.

He looked down at her, an odd glint in his eyes. "May I have your hand for this dance, Lady Winfern?"

Surprise almost took her breath away. *Everyone knows Hartford does not dance at balls.* So why was he asking? Shouldn't the man be asking Lady Edith, the only young lady to have won his attention these past two years? Theo was torn between finding an excuse to escape his presence and a rampant curiosity about what he wanted. "I haven't the least objection, Your Grace," she said, startling herself.

She placed her hand atop his arm, allowing him to guide her to join the other couples. He swept her into the waltz as the sensuous strains lifted in the air. Theo felt as if she fitted in his arms perfectly. A very silly thought to have, but there it was, nonetheless. Their elbows slid along each other, she stepped to the side, and he slid his foot along the floor, pushing her back into the intricate moves. The hand she held lightly on his shoulders flexed a bit, and she swore she felt the power of his body through his jacket and her gloves.

Theo noted he stared down at her with an expression of faint bemusement.

"I received a note from my sister a couple hours ago. I have not been able to find her since. Is this a prank conceived by you and Perdie? Punishment for my interference?"

For a moment, Theo did not understand his words, caught up in the sensation of being in the duke's arms. Many people stared at them in shock, and at the edge of the crowd, she spied Lady Edith. The girl's eyes were wide with alarm, and her gloved fingers clenched tightly onto her fan. The duke had not danced once since the start of the season. And though it was exceedingly early yet being April, that he did so now with Theo was a very unpleasant surprise to several matrons and their wards. All the scandal sheets would mention this, and the drawing rooms tomorrow would be rife with speculation.

His fingers squeezed at her elbow, tugging her gaze to him.

"You will answer me, Lady Winfern."

Something is wrong. There was a chill in his eyes that did not match the graceful and beautiful way he twirled her in the waltz. He had a quality about him that was intently compelling, dangerous. "A Prank?" Theo frowned. "I do not understand of what you speak, Your Grace."

"A few hours ago, my sister pled a headache and retired to the parlor to recover. Precisely two hours later, a footman found me and delivered a note from my sister. He was instructed to give it to me at midnight and only midnight. In that letter, she claimed she needs to live a life with meaning. Which you have graciously helped her to see."

Oh dear. "I…Your Grace, I am not certain what to say." Silently she cheered Perdie for speaking up about her wants.

"You might tell me exactly where my sister is, or you will feel my full wrath."

The icy promise had her stumbling in his embrace, but the duke's skillful spin masked her tumble, twirling her to the very edge of the crowd. Despite so many eyes on them, he managed to whisk her onto the open terrace. This would result in more than a few mentions in the scandal sheets!

"Your Grace!" Theo gasped when he deftly tugged her down the small, cobbled steps and toward the beckoning darkness of the gardens.

At the almost feral glint in his eyes, she choked her protest back down and kept pace with him until they were in an area only lit by the half-moon in the star-speckled sky. "Your Grace, what is the meaning of this?" Theo demanded the minute they stopped.

"You do not seem duly alarmed by my sister's words."

"If you do recall, Your Grace, I did mention to you that Perdie saw my townhouse as a haven for a reason."

"You were the one to encourage her down this path."

Theo frowned. "I encouraged her to share her feelings with you, yes."

"Whatever you imparted to my sister has led her to run away from her family."

Theo felt faint. "I beg your pardon?"

"You act as if you are not behind my sister's ruinous actions and the letter she left behind."

"Run away? She has run away?"

"Yes!" he snapped with such vehemence, wariness rolled down her spine in a chilly wave.

This is a disaster. "The last I spoke with Perdie was a few days ago. I advised her that until she was honest with her family about the struggles she feels, it was best she took some time away from…from our gathering."

"My sister has packed a number of her belongings and run away," he repeated icily.

"I cannot credit it!" Theo dearly hoped it was a prank. "Are you certain, Your Grace? How long ago do you think Perdie left the ball?"

"According to the butler, she went into an unmarked carriage a little over three hours ago."

An unmarked carriage. That detail suggested a

methodical plan. "Was the butler certain it was a carriage and not a hackney?"

"The man was questioned most thoroughly. It was a carriage pulled by a team of four."

"Do you have any notion where she might have headed?"

Dark grief flashed in his eyes before his expression closed off. "None. I have sent hired runners in several directions out of London and have also set people to discreetly investigate within Town."

She stared at him, wondering how he had accomplished that in such little time.

"Upon getting this letter, I launched into immediate action returning to my townhouse. Perdie was not there, and her companion Lady Felicity and her lady's maid were also missing. I have no idea in which direction they headed, and at this moment, her life might be in danger, and I do not know where she is!"

The raw emotions in his voice throbbed through her like the force of wind, pushing her to take a few steps back. Theo pressed a hand over her fiercely pounding chest. Good heavens, what was Perdie thinking to have acted with such recklessness? "I… Perdie is undoubtedly clever and capable…a young lady of good sense and…"

Theo swallowed at the anger darkening the duke's eyes, and a fresh realization dawned. "You blame *me* for…for Lady Perdita running away."

That was why he had hunted her down at this ball and asked her to dance.

His silence was his answer.

"I assure you, I have nothing to do with Perdie leaving. I do not even know the contents of the letter she left to you, Your Grace."

He unceremoniously thrust it in her face. His ill-manners piqued her ire, but Theo took the letter with trembling fingers and walked toward the lit lantern in the distance. She opened the crumpled paper and held it up to the glow of the lamp.

Dearest brother,

I have gone away for a while. It is best you do not search for me, because I am not lost. I am simply and unwaveringly decided. Lately, I feel like a blanket has been smothering me, and I dare not try and breathe around it. I need space to reflect on my thoughts and the leanings of my heart. I suspect your hand in Lady Theo turning me away from a place that has been a second home to me. My heart feels shredded, and it is through discourse with Theo I comprehend how important it is to fully understand myself, my hopes, and dreams, in regard to living my life, lest I make a mistake that I will not be able to recover from. I do not wish to live an unhappy life heavy with regrets.

This was not a decision I lightly entered. I have sold my jewelries and have fetched a very handsome sum for them. Please be assured I do have enough money to last for two years or more with some economic practice. Please know that is not to say I will be gone for that long. Miss Felicity and Hattie have accompanied me, so I am not alone. I've rented a most handsome cottage and assumed the identity of a widow to render my living alone respectable. I will also hire the proper servants for the cottage. There should be no scandal attached to me leaving London as I have not told anyone of my plans, not even my closest friends I've met since in town.

As for Lord Owen, I am not determined as yet to marry him. Please know I was very sincere in my love for him, and I still hold immeasurable love for him. I cannot ignore that he has turned a deaf ear to the desires in my heart, and I cannot continue to forge a path with a man who has so little consideration for my feelings. I implore you to cancel all matters of engagement between us, and I am sorry I could only tell you this in a letter. I feared you would insist I honor my word to marry the viscount, and I regret that I am not brave enough to face your censure and explain myself.

As soon as I am more settled, I will send you and mamma another letter. Sadly, I cannot provide you with a return address, as you will descend upon me and demand I return home. I love you, brother, and I beseech you to grant me this time so I might find my wings.

Lovingly yours, Perdie.

Theo gently folded the letter. *Oh, Perdie, what were you thinking?* It was most difficult to face the duke's ire. She stole a questioning glance at the duke, whose impassive expression now afforded her no clues. Theo's heart skipped a beat…then another. She had no words to offer him any comfort, and she suspected he would not want them. Though he tried to remain unflappable, there was a storm of emotion she could not name in his eyes.

"Your Grace"

"Until my sister has been found, you will not leave my side!"

Shock tore through Theo, rendering her speechless for several seconds. "I beg your pardon?"

CHAPTER SIX

"I am terribly sorry, Your Grace," Lady Winfern whispered, her light brown eyes luminous in the dark gardens. "But I do not understand your meaning!"

He searched for guilt or that she was hiding something. Sebastian believed this woman had helped his sister with her harebrained scheme. Perdie did not have the connections or the money to have acted alone. "I blame you entirely for this tragedy."

Her throat worked on a swallow, and her face had gone pale. "How might I assist you in recovering Perdie? I assure you my discretion in this matter is very much assured."

"You will assure more than just your discretion, my lady."

Her pulse fluttered madly, and it was clear she

was out of sorts. "What is it that you require of me, Your Grace?"

"You will not leave my sight until we have recovered my sister."

She spluttered. "I thought you jested!"

"I am entirely serious, my lady."

This time she laughed, more of a choked sound of disbelief. "You are outrageous and quite exaggerating, I am sure."

"I must disappoint you. I am not."

She considered him, her unwavering gaze searching his face. "I will do everything in my power to help you locate Lady Perdita, Your Grace. This I vow upon my honor. I will return home now, and if it is suitable, I will call upon you tomorrow at your earliest convenience."

"That will not do."

"Your Grace, it is preposterous to even suggest you will not let me from your sight. Why, that means I would have to *live* with you until your sister is found."

"You have finally seemed to grasp the situation, Lady Winfern."

She gasped and stared at him with wide, shocked eyes. "I will most certainly *not* go to your abode! Have you taken leave of your senses?"

She nibbled on her bottom lip, turning it red, a nervous gesture. Lady Winfern had a firm chin… nay, an obstinate chin and a lush pair of lips that were entirely kissable. She wore an icy blue ball-gown with pearls seeded in the hem, with a charmingly lowered décolletage. He was acutely aware of her, the soft dewiness of her skin, the delicate fragrance assailing his senses. With each shift and stir, it was as if she touched him. It infuriated Sebastian that Lady Winfern's sensual appeal should distract him at this most critical moment. Since receiving Perdie's letter, Sebastian had been in motion, setting several hired runners to track where she could have gone. The household had been in an uproar with the staff being questioned by the private runners he'd hired. No one seemed to know where his sister had gone. It was that desperate knowledge that had driven him to return to the ball to seek out this lady.

It seemed improbable Perdie could have done this on her own. A young lady of only nineteen years, who had spent most of her life pampered in Maidstone, traveling with only two other ladies, would be vulnerable to all sorts of wicked scoundrels. Their mother had collapsed but had quickly rallied, packing to leave at dawn for their estate in Maidstone in the event Perdie had gone there. This was after giving the staff a strict warning about their silence in this matter. They could not afford it to be known, for the scandal of it would ruin Perdie's reputation. Above all, Sebastian had been praying that wherever his sister had run to, she would be safe.

"Your Grace, please say something…your silence is…it is unpleasant considering it accompanies that fierce scowl."

Sebastian wasted no time reaffirming that she would not leave his side. He prowled toward her, grabbed her around the waist, dipped and swung her into his arms. The lady was still only for a heartbeat before an outraged squeak came from her and a mad struggle. "Be still, or I might accidentally drop you."

She clutched at his shoulders, and it befuddled him why her soft weight against his chest felt so incredibly pleasant.

"Do you want to start a scandal? Someone might see us! How would you explain me being in your arms?" she asked faintly.

"I am Hartford; who would dare question me?"

"Your arrogance is astounding, but I referred to my reputation!"

He stopped walking. "There is no one about this part of the garden. If you come quietly, I will set you down."

"And if I am not biddable?"

"I will continue as we are, and damn the consequences to hell."

She took a steady breath. "I will not fuss."

Sebastian lowered her to the ground. The top of her head barely brushed his chin, and he was tempted to lean in to inhale the fragrance emanating from her. Instead, he stepped back, took her gloved hand within his, and continued walking toward the side entrance.

She attempted to tug her hand from his to no avail. "Your Grace, surely you know even this will see the tongues wagging and see our names linked in the scandal sheets for weeks! I will not attempt to escape if that is what you are outrageous enough to think."

Seb made no reply, and she muttered something beneath her breath about him being insufferable. His carriage waited where he had left it with the explicit instructions that he would only be inside a few minutes. They exited the garden, and his footmen hurried to knock the steps down for her. Sebastian helped her inside the cozy equipage and settled his frame in the seat opposite to her. The carriage rumbled into motion, and it was several moments before she spoke.

"I've left my coat."

"I'm sure the countess will discreetly return it to you, Lady Winfern."

She stared at him in the dim light of the carriage, her hands folded demurely into her lap. *What an act.* "I suspect that you aided my sister in hatching this dangerous plan. You know her precise location, for you helped her find those accommodations," Sebastian said, studying every nuance of her expression. "I will have her location."

Her breath caught at his implication, a flush warming her cheeks. "I would never allow Perdie to act in such a reckless manner. You mistake my character, Your Grace."

Sincerity dwelt in her voice, and her eyes implored him to believe her. Frustratingly he did, but what if this was all an act? How could Perdie have put such a scheme together by herself? He made no other accusation, and the lady was content for them to travel in silence. Several minutes passed before the lady was inspired to push aside the carriage curtain to peek outside.

"You are not taking me home."

"I believe I mentioned you will not leave my side until my sister is recovered."

Her lips parted, but no words came forth. And Sebastian felt an inordinate amount of satisfaction that he had robbed her of speech.

"Where are you taking me, Your Grace?"

"To my home."

"I…and what will we do there?"

"I plan to go to bed early to get a proper rest for the journey tomorrow."

"What journey?"

"To wherever my sister might have fled. It is tempting to dash out into the night to start the mad search for my sister but given the rain, and that you must travel with me, that would be idiocy."

"I shall travel with you?"

How young she looked with her eyes so rounded and her hands resting against her throat.

"You will bear this burden with me until she is found. Please follow along, Lady Winfern. I do not like repeating myself."

A sound, very much like a croak, came from her throat, and he bit back his smile. It mildly shocked him that he felt the need to smile, given the circumstances.

"Very well, Your Grace. I am acquiescing without a quarrel not only to assure you that I have nothing to do with her disappearance but because I care for Perdie very much."

Once again, sincerity suffused her voice, but Sebastian was not moved. If she had not inveigled herself into his sister's life and planted those ridiculous notions in her head, this problem would not exist. Reading his sister's letter and the implication behind her words had nearly crushed the breath from his lungs. Somewhere during the eleven years he had acted as a father to Perdie, he must have failed her or let her down abominably for her to believe she had to hide whatever she endured. A young girl on her own without much protection would be very tempting and easy prey for many miscreants. Sebastian would find her at any cost, and the woman before him might have helped his sister to run away. He did not trust her to tell him the truth if she had. The lady clearly had a rebellious spirit and would likely encourage his sister to act improperly.

No, Sebastian would not let Lady Theodosia Winfern from his sight.

CHAPTER SEVEN

*L*ess than thirty minutes after departing Prue's home, Theo climbed the winding stairs to the landing of the second floor of the duke's townhouse situated in Grosvenor Square. It seemed incredible that she was under the man's roof. The butler had appeared quite shocked by her presence, but he had quickly recovered. The rest of the household appeared to be abed, and the duke had bid her follow him up the stairs.

He stopped at an impressive oak door, but he made no move to twist the knob. Instead, he turned to face Theo, his gaze sweeping over her in a quick but very thorough appraisal. "You will sleep in my chamber tonight."

Theo was persuaded that she must have misunderstood *entirely.* "I do beg your pardon, Your Grace. Surely you will not occupy the same space… or the same bed?"

The darkening of his eyes sent another ripple of shock through Theo, for within their depths, she spied a flash of desire. "I do not believe my nerves can endure any more surprises," she cried.

His lashes lowered, and when those eyes met hers again, all traces of want vanished. Had she imagined it?

"Must I truly repeat myself again, Lady Winfern?"

She choked on her gasp of outrage. "Your Grace! I will most certainly not sleep in your private chamber. I will not slink away in the night if that is your fear."

"It is exactly that, my lady."

Her heart pounded, and her breathing turned rapid. "I suspect you are trying to shock my sensibilities as some sort of punishment for what you imagined I did."

"Never that," he said drily. "We can end this charade now if you tell me exactly how you helped my sister to leave town. Or is she still in town? Is she at a private home of yours?"

Theo scoffed. "You goading me with your outrageous suggestions will not prompt me to give you a different answer."

And she did understand how alarmingly suspicious it appeared. With a huff, she whirled around and started to march away. If he dared to think she would spend a minute in his chamber, he was sorely mistaken. *The scoundrel!* He was taking his gamble too far. Theo stopped at the door a few paces down and tested the handle. It opened into a room that gave the impression of largeness and open space. Without any fire lit in the hearth or gas lamp, she could not decipher if it was a guest bedroom. Before she could step inside, someone lifted her from behind.

She wriggled like a fish on a hook, but the duke only tightened his arms about her. Theo growled low in her throat, and a sound suspiciously like a chuckle emitted from the man.

"Set me down this instance, or you will face my wrath and let me assure you it is formidable."

His steps faltered for a moment, and she glared up at him. The duke was not deterred, and soon they were in his room, the door slamming behind them. He deposited Theo on her feet, but she was already jumping from his embrace. She gaped at him when he locked the door and pocketed the key.

Narrowing her eyes, she strolled toward him. "You underestimate me, Your Grace."

An arrogant brow lifted. "A lesser woman would have surely descended into throes of nervous spasms or swooning fits by now, so I suspect I might truly find myself in a position to worry about your formidable wrath; however, you will stay in this room where I can keep a watchful—"

Moving with speed, she hooked her feet at his ankle and deftly twisted. The duke went down, twisting with agility to break his fall. He too was trained in the art of fighting, and unexpectedly the knowledge thrilled Theo. Before she could dance back from his reach, he grabbed one of her knees and tugged. "Your Grace," she cried as her feet vanished from beneath her.

The brute! She braced for the impact, except she didn't slam into the ground as she had expected, but onto a very solid and muscular chest as they rolled to a stop on the carpet. Theo's face was pressed into the curve of his throat, one of her legs draped across his thighs, the other thankfully on the floor. She was maddeningly conscious of her body on top of his, that she could feel the press of his length…and muscles against her softness. The breadth of his shoulders seemed to surround her. The duke hadn't seemed so overpoweringly male or muscular a few minutes ago. An odd feeling of awareness and vulnerability cascaded over her senses, and she curled her fingers into the carpet by his head.

Theo swallowed, alarmingly savoring the feeling of being surrounded by him. Her heart felt as if it had stopped. *This is reckless madness*. The thought beat restlessly at her, yet she did not want to push away from it. With a sense of astonishment, she wondered if this was what desire felt like. This hot weak feeling low in her belly, the odd flutter in her heart, and the surge of hunger, as if she smelled Mrs. Gooden making ice-cream using one of Frederick Nutt's delightful recipes. She wanted to lick the duke. Theo almost dissolved into a giggle at the very improper and unexpected thought.

"Are you hurt?" he gruffly asked.

Theo's heart started beating again, if unevenly. She pressed a palm against his chest and pushed herself up, only to freeze. The intensity with which the duke stared at her made Theo's body feel flushed and unfamiliar. "I...I am not hurt, Your Grace."

"Perhaps it is time you call me, Seb...or Sebastian should you prefer it."

It was unbearably tempting to press her nose into the crook of his neck and inhale his rich masculine scent. "You may continue calling me, Lady Winfern," she muttered crossly, annoyed that his nearness wreaked havoc on her senses.

His eyes widened before crinkling at the corner. The duke chuckled, the rich and very warm sound rolling through her and filling low in her belly with strange fluttering. The duke's eyes lost their cold and rather arrogant expression. Now they were heated with humor...and desire.

That desire hooked something low in her belly and sharply pulled. He seemed aware of her fear, of her hot, flushed skin and acutely sensitive nerves. Unexpectedly, he lifted a hand to her forehead, where he tenderly brushed aside a few curled tendrils. Theo must have looked a fright with her mass of hair tumbling from her upswept chignon.

"You are a very surprising woman, Lady

Winfern. Not many men could have brought me down with such effortless skill. I am impressed."

"My friend once suggested a fabled dragon was easier to find than a progressive-minded gentleman. I am impressed that you are impressed."

She attempted to roll off him, but he went with her so that he was now the one above her. Theo clasped his shoulders, gripping his jacket as if it were a lifeline. "Your Grace…"

"Are you spoken for?"

Astonished, Theo peered up at the duke. What did he mean? She searched his face, her heart pounding. "Are you asking me if I have a lover, Your Grace?"

"Yes."

She stared at him for endless seconds. The duke did not prod or push but waited with surprising patience. "I have no lover." Theo did not know why she answered such an intimate question.

"Good," he murmured.

Her belly went hot. "I suspect you wish to kiss me, considering the manner you are staring at my mouth," she whispered.

Theo was wretchedly, horrifyingly tempted.

The duke appeared faintly surprised. "Are you always this direct?"

"Would you prefer if I had been coy?"

The beginning of a smile raised the corners of his mouth. "No."

"I too have wondered what it might feel like to

kiss you, Your Grace," she confessed without any embarrassment.

His eyes darkened. "How often have you wondered?"

She flushed, and her lips parted. Determined to appear worldly and indifferent, she murmured, "Isn't that the nature of curiosity? That the idea tease and torment our senses until we know the truth of our musings?"

Lady Lucinda, another widowed friend greatly admired for her sophisticated charm, would be most proud of Theo at this moment. "Best we get it over with and out of the way since we will be traveling together in our search for Perdie, and we would not want this…this curiosity to affect us on our journey."

His eyes widened slightly. "Get it out of the way…, no sweet words to cajole my lips to yours, Lady Winfern?"

"You require flattery to your conceit for a mere kiss…how duke like," she said mockingly.

"You have a barbed tongue," he said. "How lowering to a man's vanity."

"Be careful; I might lick you with it," she retorted, shocking herself silly at that rejoinder. Theo felt as if she were wholly another creature. She did not flirt, nor did she taunt provocatively. This was not her, had never been her, yet something she had never known to be a part of herself purred deep inside, stretched, reaching for something…

something this man owned. The awareness shook her.

With an enormous effort of will, she held his stare which beheld her as if she were endlessly fascinating. His gaze traveled up to the large four-poster bed hovering in their periphery amidst a masculine décor and then back to her in leisurely invitation. "I believe you will make me an excellent bed partner."

A sweet twisting ache stirred in her belly, and her heart quickened at the temptation lurking in his wicked stare. "I am not looking for a lover."

Something flashed in the blue depths of his gaze. "Are you most certain, Lady Winfern?"

"I am."

Genuine regret chased his face before his expression shuttered. "Ah, a pity that, it would have made our traveling much more pleasant."

"I am much more than a pleasant diversion for any man, Your Grace."

"Did I mention you would sweat, scream, rake me with your nails, and twist beneath me or on top of me from the agony of pleasure to be had from my fingers…tongue, and cock at least twice every night?"

Theo almost fainted at that provocative question which hit her in the belly like a bolt of heat. "Sounds like too much effort that, all that twisting."

The duke chuckled, his eyes lighting with an

indefinable emotion. "You *are* most interesting, Lady Winfern."

A spurt of humor rushed through her. How unusual it all was. A week ago, she did not know this man, and now she was in his chamber, pinned beneath his bulk in the most scandalous fashion, hearing a most indiscreet proposal. And she wasn't at all afraid he would ravish her. In truth, she found their bantering…titillating. *To be the duke's lover…* The very idea set a path of fire down her throat and into her stomach. "You may call me Theodosia…or Theo."

"Theodosia," he murmured. The duke's fingertips fluttered across her skin…downward over her lips, his touch lingering and arousing. "Let's get this pesky curiosity out of the way, shall we?"

Her chest lifted on a harsh breath. What idiocy was she indulging in, remaining sprawled beneath the duke, her thighs perfectly cradling his weight? She was a woman with woman needs and yearnings. Clearly, her body and heart were tired of suppressing them.

He touched the corner of her mouth. "Has your curiosity dampened?"

She almost averted her gaze from his measuring scrutiny. "No," she answered honestly. *It had grown in unchecked leaps and bounds.*

He dipped his head and passionately caught her mouth with his in a searing kiss. Theo's heartbeat quickened. Tendrils of alarm and excitement speared through her stomach. He tasted her gently…sweetly.

It was so very unexpectedly wonderful—her very first kiss.

The tip of his tongue barely brushed hers before it withdrew. Theo moaned at the feel of his mouth against hers, at the taste of whisky. Hardly able to believe her wild recklessness, Theo bit into his lower lip, then licked the spot to soothe it. Sebastian slanted his mouth over hers, nipping at her bottom lip before licking the seam of her mouth. Need broke over her, warm, rich, stirring a tide of longing which had long been buried. She curled her hands around his neck, holding him close to her, as she passionately satisfied her curiosity.

THE TASTE OF THEODOSIA, wild and heady, flooded Sebastian's senses with such wicked want and hunger. As he deepened the kiss, his tongue flicked at her lips for entry, and she made a soft, hungry sound against his mouth before parting her lips to his entreaty. Their kiss almost felt…artless. Her mouth beneath his moved with tentative passion, and it aroused his ardor to an astonishing degree.

Their tongues touched, she sighed, and he groaned. He swore the lady tasted sweet…and innocently carnal if there was such a thing.

Sebastian was tempted to push up her petticoats and dress, tug her drawers to the side, and bury his aching cock into the wet tightness he suspected he'd find. He wanted her with an unfamiliar and disquieting urgency. He reached between them, trailing his fingers up the length of her leg and over her silken stockings. A hot gasp rushed from her mouth to his, and he swallowed it, sucking on her tongue with carnal greed, allowing his fingers to dance closer to her quim. He shifted his hands so that his knuckles brushed against her sex through her drawers. *Fucking hell.* She was damp and heated, and with a little twist of her hips, she opened her legs wider.

An invitation to touch…to perhaps slip a finger deep inside her body and test her readiness. Seb ran his knuckles over her drawers once more, this time pressing them firmer against her sex. The drawers got wetter, and he groaned. She was sweetly responsive and hungry. Perfect, for he damn well felt as if he were about to spend in his trousers like an untried lad.

A violent shudder worked through her body, and she pulled her mouth from his. "Stop," she murmured.

It was a mere whisper of sound, but he pulled his hand away immediately and rolled from her to lay beside her on the carpet. His heart pounded like he had run around the vast lawn of his estate. He very badly wanted to bed the woman beside him.

Stunned at his unruly response, Seb cleared his throat. "I forgot myself for a moment. Forgive me."

She was silent for several beats, then replied, "I…I believe our curiosity has been satisfied."

Far from it. His cock was so painfully hard, he felt it would spill through his damn front fall. Sebastian almost felt embarrassed by his unchecked desires. He turned his head on the carpet, not surprised to find she had done the same and was staring at him. Her lips glistened red and wet. They were swollen, proof of how thoroughly he had kissed her. Her lovely golden eyes, framed by incredibly long lashes, looked dismayed, even horrified, by the depth of her reactions to him.

Yes…you were wanton and eager for me as I were for you. Do not shy away from it. But you do not want a lover. Unexpectedly he felt like a cad, and with a harsh breath, he jerked into a sitting position. What the hell had he been thinking to kidnap her from a ball, force her to his house, and then into his private chambers? *Bloody hell.* He was conducting his search of Perdie with alarming indiscretion. Surprisingly, there was no complaint from Theodosia. She had borne his cavalier treatment with aplomb. A rush of admiration for her mettle filled him. Sebastian had truly departed of his good and honorable senses, which had guided him since his father died and entrusted so many precious things into his keeping.

"I will take you home," he said abruptly, glancing down at her.

Her eyes widened, and her chest lifted on a deep breath. "I…thank you, Your Grace. I believe that might be best."

Her tender mouth looked exquisitely swollen.

"I've been a beast and I apologize."

It was clear she had not expected his apology and perhaps did not know what to make of it. A small smile touched her lips, but wariness lingered in her gaze and questions about what had just happened. "Are you sorry for kidnapping me or for satisfying your curiosity so lustily?"

He might never get used to the directness of her manner. "Kidnapping you." No scenario on this earth could inspire him to regret kissing her. Sebastian had never indulged in a kiss quite so satisfying or one that had aroused all his senses so completely.

"You are forgiven."

He arched a brow, and she smiled, a dimple peeking in her cheek. *How charming.*

"Upon my honor, I will aid you in searching for Perdie. I shall not run from this responsibility, and I doubt there is anywhere I could run that you would not find me."

He nodded, reaching out to push a tendril that had escaped her chignon behind her ears. A delicate shudder went through her frame, and he felt the answering call deep inside his body. Her enjoyment of his kiss hadn't been so wild and visceral because he had been ruthless in his persuasion. The attraction wasn't one-sided. And he had gone much further than she anticipated. He was a man of control; he should have stopped at a simple kiss. "Theodosia, I will also apologize for what just happened, I—"

His throat closed when she placed two fingers over his mouth.

"I am not a debutante fit to swoon because you kissed me, Your Grace. I quite enjoyed it."

Said so boldly, but there was a touch of shyness in her eyes that stirred something tender and foreign inside him. He pulled back sharply from the sensation, frowning down at her. "I overstepped your boundaries, and it is for that I sincerely apologize."

"I wasn't brainlessly swept away by passion. I was aware of every touch…I stopped you when I was ready to do so," she said with an arrogant curl to her lips.

Sebastian got the impression she wanted to appear a confident vixen. Still, in her lovely eyes, he spied an intangible emotion, and he suddenly wished he knew her well enough to understand what she might be feeling. He pushed to his feet and held out his hand to her. When she took it, he gently pulled her to her feet.

"Your graciousness, I will not forget."

A brief smile flickered at her mouth, and she stared at him as if he were an enigma.

"If you give me a few minutes, I will send for

the carriage." Sebastian walked away, quite aware of her eyes following his departure. Another unknown sensation shuddered inside his chest. He did not like it at all. Sebastian could afford no diversions in the form of a sensually appealing woman he was growing curious about. For the first time, he wondered at the logic of taking her with him. He quickly brushed that aside, for he had not exculpated her from his suspicions.

CHAPTER EIGHT

*T*he very next morning, Theo swung her legs over the side of the bed and pulled on her warm dressing gown. Though a few weeks ago spring had announced its wonderful presence with some sunshine, blooming flowers, and melting snow, the last few days had been unusually wet from the rain. After cinching the robe, she hurried to her armoire. There would be no delay in packing and readying for the duke to send his carriage for her. While taking her home last night, he had asked her to be ready with her bags by nine. If he needed her at his side because he did not trust her, by his side she would remain. Theo did not want the duke as an enemy. Not when he knew about her club and had already once promised he could take it apart, brick by brick. *The beast…albeit a most wonderfully kissing beast.*

She rang for her lady's maid, and with a few

quick instructions to Molly, the packing started. Theo also sent a footman with a note to deliver to Prue, Charity and Lucinda, the club members who were more like family than anything else. A quick reply came from Lucinda saying she was abed with a most dreadful cold after being caught in a downpour yesterday. No other note returned to her, so Theo anticipated her friends would soon arrive.

Lady Charity Rutherford, sister to Earl Bonham, barged into her bedroom almost an hour later, her gaze surveying the clothes on the chaise longue and on the bed. "I came as soon as I got your note. Luckily, I was already dressed for a ride in the park."

Charity and Theo shared a closer age and had similar interests. They were closer to each other than Prue, who was four years their junior. Charity wore a large hat she'd designed herself and was terribly out of fashion. It served primarily to protect her fair skin from the sun. She had the loveliest auburn hair, which had been coifed to allow several tendrils to curl at her temples and along her neck. Her eyes were the most vivid green, and Charity often bemoaned her fair and quick to freckled skin. Many had remarked that she was an unexceptional bluestocking, more concerned with her inventions than anything else. She was Theo's dearest friend and her fourth partner in crime in running the lady's club.

"What is going on, Theo?" Charity asked with a

small frown. "You seem very out of sorts, and that is not like you."

Before she could reply, another knock sounded, and Prue sallied inside. "Good, you are already here, Charity. I daresay I would not have been able to wait on you to catch up with the gossip. Lucinda has a cold, so she will not make it!" She rounded on Theo. "I still cannot believe you danced with the Duke of Hartford last night!"

Charity gasped. "What?"

"Yes," Prue said, dropping into the chaise to repose against the cushions. "He also whisked her outside in the gardens, and our dearest Theo did not return inside. I suspect all the scandal sheets will mention it. I've already instructed a maidservant to procure me all the copies, even the notorious ones!"

"I cannot credit you are on friendly terms with the duke," Charity said. "He seems very haughty and lacking in any sort of humor, not the sort of gentleman you usually favor."

Quickly Theo relayed *most* of what had transpired for the evening.

"You are doing what?" Prue demanded in shocked tones.

"I will be traveling with the duke for…I do not know how long. Until Lady Perdie is located."

"*The* Duke of Hartford?"

"Yes."

"And Lady Perdie is his sister?" Charity

demanded. "Why ever did you not tell us that is why you turned her away?"

Theo whirled around. "Will you repeat everything I said in this exaggerated manner?"

Charity scowled. "Yes! Until I understand the matter at hand."

Prue interjected, "You cannot travel alone with the duke after last night. If this is to be known… yours and the duke's absence left everyone in a fine twitter. I am certain the scandal sheets will be linking your names together for *weeks*."

Theo groaned and flopped onto the bed, staring at the canopy. "I do not think His Grace thought beyond his anger and fear for his sister. I could hardly sleep last night for wondering where Perdie could have gone. How could she have been so reckless? What if she is hurt? What if she trusted the wrong person in this mad scheme of hers?"

Of course, neither Prue nor Charity could answer her demands; the only sound in the large chamber was the crackling fire in the hearth.

Charity sauntered over to lay beside her. "Theo?"

"Yes."

"I, too, am worried for Perdie, but we know her to be a very smart and quick-thinking girl. She would not have acted without planning."

"That is what I am dearly hoping."

"It is still very risky to your reputation to travel

alone with the duke," Charity bemoaned with a sigh.

Theo pushed into a sitting position on the edge of the bed. "I feel myself under an obligation to help him. I…if not for me and this very club, would Perdie have acted in such an irresponsible manner? I will risk it, but I will be very careful to remain veiled. If anyone should see the duke traveling with a lady, they might only question the mysterious nature of it." Theo stood, walked over to the table by the window and took up a few books she had been reading to put in her valise.

"I want to know something if you will grant me your undivided attention," Prue said.

Theo glanced at Prue, who was now sitting up on the chaise, her eyes twinkling with something naughty. "What is it?" Theo asked, glancing between her two friends.

"Why are your lips swollen?"

Theo raised her fingers to her lips, shocked to feel her cheeks heating as if she were a girl in the schoolroom. "Are they swollen?"

"Yes," they cried together.

"The duke kissed me," she whispered.

"I knew it! The way he looked at you last night was not all about his sister," Prue cried triumphantly.

"You speak nonsense; this kiss was born from the duke being irritated and was more likely

wanting to tease me…or distress my sensibilities."
And curiosity.

"I suppose you showed him you are made of stern stuff," Charity said with a light laugh.

Theo's breath caught remembering the feel and taste of him. She lied to herself about what he felt. The raw intensity of his stare promised Theo something she inexplicably wanted. His kiss…his touch…perhaps even his ravishment. He'd tempted her with a passion she had never experienced but had felt low in her belly in her dreams. Those indecent yearnings once again welled from a place deep within Theo. What would it be like to have a lover, for a man's body to move inside hers? Would it end the emptiness and the loneliness, or would it only fill it for a brief moment in time?

Should she trust him with her body, would he marry her after if she were even amenable to such a suit? *Surely not*. The Duke of Hartford was rumored to have an alliance with a most sought-after debutante in the ton. A great heiress, a beauty, with apparently an impeccable character. If Theo were to give in to the burning lust in his gaze, it would only be for an affair. There had been a time in her life Theo had felt desperate to live, to have adventures, to feel passion. Theo had been so young and frightened when she'd married Viscount Winfern, a man who was two and sixty. She had wanted to experience life to the fullest with the boy she had admired, but it was not meant to be. "That the duke might desire me means very little."

"I think what is most important is that you want him in return."

With a gasp, she glanced at Charity, who stared at Theo somberly. Had she been so transparent with her thoughts?

"Is it safe to travel alone with him?"

"I shall be perfectly fine. I am not about to fall at the duke's feet and offer myself for his ravishment."

"Perhaps you should," a voice said behind her.

"Prue!"

"Wouldn't that deal with the pesky problem of your innocence?"

At this moment, she almost regretted telling her dearest friends the truth of her marriage. "I am not an innocent."

"But you remain untouched."

"It is not a pesky problem that needs the solution of a lover," she retorted.

A faraway look entered Prue's eyes. "And don't you want to know the touch of a gentleman? What it is like to be someone's lover?"

"I am not about to embark on an affair, especially with a man as powerful as the duke. That is akin to placing my head in a lion's mouth."

Charity touched her shoulder. "I've never known you to be so flustered. That means you *are* tempted by him."

"I am also tempted to eat ice cream every day. You do not see me badgering Mrs. Dwyer to follow Mr. Nutt's recipes and make me all the ice cream I can devour."

Prue scoffed, and it embarrassed Theo her friend might think her to be a coward. "Even as a woman of some means and independence, I still linger under the scrutiny of society."

"You were never afraid of society before," Charity pointed out with a meaningful glance about the room.

"Then *you* go and have a bloody affair with the Duke of Hartford," Theo snapped, thoroughly vexed.

Abashed by her rebuke, Prue hurried over to her. "Forgive us, Theo, for being so pushy. It is…I have never seen your eyes so bright with interest."

And Theo suspected her friend was delicate with her choice of words. Had she really been so transparent with her desires?

"I know you both mean well, and I love you for it, but I must be careful in my dealings with the duke. They shall remain businesslike at all times. He has warned me more than once that I should not like him for an enemy. I believe him. I risk too much, our club, the life we enjoy now, to entangle with him. I am not interested in a dalliance of any kind, and if I were, it would not be with a gentleman like Hartford."

She felt quite out of good humor with her

friends because their teasing provoked thoughts and erotic images best left in the dark of one's chamber. The loneliness which often came unbidden swept through her then, and she blew out a soft sigh. She had felt no desire for marriage and had eschewed all thoughts of romance or an affair. Theo had directed her purse and efforts into building another life, one that was meaningful for her. The idea for the club had been born from the close friendship she shared with Charity and Lucinda.

They had been such a comfort during the many lonely days of her marriage. Many would not comprehend that her husband had never kissed her or even attempted to consummate their marriage. It had been a blessing to Theo who had been a frightened and shy seventeen-year-old girl in the early months. In the later months, it had been the beginning of solitude and a longing for something she hardly understood. Despite the many rumors of mistresses, the viscount had been impotent. Marrying someone as pretty and youthful as her had been a recommendation from a doctor. The viscount had still died without issue and a distant cousin, a very amiable gentleman, had inherited the viscounty. Shrugging aside those old memories, she stood. "I am trying to pack as lightly as possible. A few day dresses, my specially made riding habits, a pelisse or two, and perhaps an evening gown or two." Theo was deceiving herself; she would need a lot more than that.

Prue held up a newly made evening gown thoughtfully. "You should have your lady's maid accompany you."

"You forget I am past the age of need for a chaperone, and I am a widow." Though her hair would be very hard to manage by herself. "I believe I shall indeed take Molly along with me. I have no notion how arduous traveling with the duke will be, but surely he will provide a comfortable carriage."

"Theo?"

She turned, facing Charity absentmindedly. "Yes?"

"I *dare* you," Charity said softly.

Theo faltered, truly shocked that it was Charity daring her and not Prue. "Charity!"

"I *dare* you to be wicked with the duke. I dare you to allow him kisses and liberties and to just live for yourself. I dare you if you are tempted by him, to steal a slice of happiness and comfort that you often deny yourself while you care for others. I dare you when he least expects it, to kiss the duke."

CHAPTER NINE

*T*he large conveyance in which Theo had been traveling for the better part of a day rolled to a stop along a gravel-lined driveway. She parted the carriage curtain to see the duke dismounting from his impressive stallion to issue orders to a stable lad, and the innkeeper who had hurried out of his establishment to greet him. It seemed the duke was a frequent and well-respected patron of this inn.

"Have we reached our destination, milady?" Molly asked, her eyes bright with curiosity.

"I believe so," Theo replied, looking about the courtyard of a large and well-built inn constructed in the Tudor style with its half-timbered walls, sweeping entrance and casement windows made up of small, mulled panes.

Sebastian walked over to the carriage, and she rose from the seat as the door opened, allowing him to assist her down the steps. A warm feeling blossomed through her when he extended the same considerations to a blushing Molly.

"Thank you," Theo said glancing around the well-presented inn. "Where are we headed, Your Grace?"

He hadn't provided much information earlier when they departed town, and she had been content with avoiding him for the first few hours, the memory of their torrid kiss too fresh in her mind and in the very air around them whenever their gazes collided.

"Brighton. We visit a seaside resort yearly since our father died. I bought a house close by last year. I am hoping this is where Perdie has gone."

They walked toward the large doorway and the portly gentleman waiting to greet them which he did effusively. It seemed the duke was known. They made their way inside the inn, which had only a handful of patrons in the common area.

Theo wondered if Sebastian would procure them two rooms. They had traveled for the entire day with little conversation between them to pass the time. She had smartly fitted lacy veils to her hats giving herself a mysterious air should they encounter anyone from their Society in their travels. Though she was a widow and by society's rules was afforded more freedom than debutantes and young ladies, Theo was still careful knowing a ruined reputation would negatively impact those who joined her at 48 Berkeley Square.

The innkeeper slid an indiscreet glance at her then quickly shifted his attention to the Duke.

"Your Grace," the innkeeper began tentatively. "We are at occupancy. It is only the one room we have available, Your Grace?"

"It will do," he replied with no inflection in his voice.

That flutter once again went off in Theo's belly and she was grateful the veil hid her expression.

"Very well, Your Grace," the innkeeper said, handing him a key. "It is the only room on the third floor with ample privacy."

The duke then secured a few of the common rooms reserved for servants for her lady's maid, his footmen, and coachmen traveling only a few minutes behind in another conveyance with their luggage.

"Will you be heading down for supper or will you take a tray in your room?" the innkeeper's wife asked, bustling over and also introducing herself as Mrs. Chambers.

The duke glanced at Theo.

"A tray in the room, thank you," she murmured.

The innkeeper's wife led the way up the stairs to an impressive room surprisingly well-furnished, with a large bed flushed near the windows draped with billowing green brocade.

"Hot water will be sent up, mi lady," Mrs.

Chambers brightly said. "And a tray of roast mutton chops, bakcd potatoes, and shepherd pie. The best in the area."

"Thank you," Theo said warmly.

The lady bustled from the room with a jaunt in her step, leaving Theo alone with the duke and her lady's maid.

"I have no need of you Molly for the rest of the evening. I am fully able to manage a bath and dressing. Go and have your rest and finish the gothic romance you've hidden in your skirts."

Molly smiled and dipped into a quick curtsy. "Thank you, milady." Turning to the duke, she did the same, and hurried from the room.

The duke sauntered over to the windows overlooking the back gardens of the inn. Thunder rumbled in the sky, a portend of the rain to come. He looked starkly uncompromising and alone. She couldn't look at him without feeling that irregular skip in her heartbeat. *And why should it beat so for you when it has never done so for any man?* Theo was certain that a mere glance at her face should let the duke know that the memory of their kiss haunted her for every moment of the day. She wondered if it was the same for him, or had his curiosity satisfied itself?

"Your Grace—"

"You may go ahead and eat without me. I am going out for a walk." There was a starkness in his eyes when he faced her.

"It is about to rain," she said, glancing beyond his shoulder to the overcast sky.

"So it is," he said, taking his leave of her and the room.

Theo stared at the closed door, wondering if she should follow him. *And say what?* He had not invited her into his confidence. The duke was clearly not kindly disposed toward her, and she was with him for only one reason—he believed her a schemer who very well knew where his sister hid.

With a sigh, Theo pulled the veil and hat from her head, unpinning her hair and allowing it to tumble to her hips in heavy waves. The day had been long, the journey tiring, and she was dirty from travel. The promised bath and a well-prepared meal were most welcoming. Instead of moving behind the screen toward the left corner of the room to start undressing, Theo walked over to the window and looked down.

The rain had started falling in earnest, a few newcomers were scurrying inside while the stable lads hurriedly led horses and carriages away to unharness and comfortably set them up in the stables. Only the duke walked toward the forest edging the property. Theo pressed her hands to the cool glass of the windows, leaning forward a bit. He did not disappear into the woods but stood with both his hands fisted at his hips, his face tilted to the heavens while the rain poured over him.

"The silly man will catch his death," she

muttered, an ache rising inside her heart. "Oh, Perdie, even if he were totally uncompromising surely you must have known your disappearance would have wrecked your brother." Theo had not thought her a young lady of selfish sensibilities.

The duke turned around, and their gazes collided. Theo jerked back, flushing that she had been caught ogling him so blatantly. Moving tentatively, she leaned forward to see if he had moved away. Her breath caught, he was still staring up at their window, an indefinable expression on his handsome face. Swallowing down her mortification, she lifted a hand in a small wave. He did not return the gesture, and she stepped away, drawing the dark curtains close, shutting out the duke, and the unexpected temptations rising inside.

What would it be like to have a lover? To have someone touch her…hold her in the nights when it was cold and lonely…to be kissed and cherished. As if controlled by another, Theo's fingers fluttered to her lips and pressed.

Dares are so horribly tempting.

Almost an hour after leaving Theodosia alone, Sebastian opened the door to their chamber to find her reclining atop the well-padded bed, her lovely hair covered by a lace cap, and laying on her side with her knees drawn up. She looked so fresh faced and young he wondered at her age. The lady seemed too young to be a widow and a woman of the world. To his mind, she barely looked older than his sister in the way she curled into herself to sleep.

An odd rush of affection went through him, and with a frown he glanced away, sat on the armchair by the fire and tugged off his wet boots. Earlier a wild feeling of being trapped had risen up inside to wrap its ugly arms around him. The last time he'd felt that well of sensations he hardly knew how to process had been when his father died. It had been imperative to escape into the falling rain.

Seb felt soaked to the bones, and the two glass of brandy he had in the inn's dining area had done little to warm him. Unexpectedly he felt weary, another damned feeling to add to the constant worry and pain hooked like a barb inside his chest. Dropping his boot with a tug, he froze when Theodosia murmured something sleepily, and shifted her position, turning her back to him.

Sharing a room with her might prove to be inconvenient for he would not allow his valet inside to assist him. Seb really should have procured a private room for her, instead of allowing any shade to be cast on her reputation if they were found to be traveling together.

Staring at her, he wondered if the witty lady he'd kissed senseless could be deceiving him still about his sister's whereabouts? He made the mental note that going forward, they would not share a room. That way, the stirring inside might be unlikely to manifest its irritating head.

The nightgown she wore hid her shape but that only served to fuel his wayward thoughts. It drew taut across her backside and tangled around her legs. What did she look like underneath the voluminous material? He itched to part the gown so he could learn the shape and weight of her full breasts, the softness of her belly and move down to the delightfully rounding of her hips, and then to the heated valley of her sex. Sebastian could imagine the flavor of her sweet little quim when he tasted her and her wild response. It would be like when he'd sucked her tongue into his mouth. That hot little purr she'd made, that eager arch into his embrace already told him she'd be the most delightful lover.

With a scoff of irritation, he stood and made his way behind the screen and undressed. He quickly undressed and tugged on night leggings and a banyan to protect her modesty. Lying on the bed, the mattress dipped, and she muttered again. The lady was not a serene sleeper at all, and he smiled, thinking even in sleep she could be thorny. This would be an experience for him, sleeping with a woman in his bed for the full night. Even with his past lovers, Seb had always been concerned about going home before dawn. His family had been the most important thing in his world view. Whenever he visited town for Parliament, he did not linger once the sessions were over but often returned to Maidstone to be with his sister and mother. A few times he would paint the town with his friends, indulging in some wicked and carnal pursuits but he'd never allowed himself to be consumed with trivialities like some of his counterparts.

Theodosia shifted, and to his shock, she rolled twice coming up to his side and snuggling close. His chest lifted on a surprised breath. *What the hell?* He took his time in glancing down at her laced cap head. *Was this how you slept with your husband? Curling into his side as if you are hiding from the world and seeking shelter?*

He doubted it, the old viscount had been a great orator on the floor of Parliament and they normally stood on the same side when it came to passing bills and fighting for more rights for the poor and disenfranchised. The man had however been addicted to vice—frequenting several gambling houses in the underbelly of London, and also rumored to have kept several mistresses. It was a wonder he had gotten married to this lady, though her beauty might have been the thing to reel him to her side.

Temptation beat at Seb to drag Theodosia across his body and seduce her with ruthless kisses and filthy promises of the ways he would make her release. He knew his skill as a lover, and it would only take a few minutes to have her squirming with burning lust. Seb gripped the pillow above his head, breathing easily to soothe the pounding ache in his heart and cock.

She rolled from his side, kicking at the tangled sheets around her feet. Inexplicably he knew the moment she came awake. The rhythm of her breathing changed, and a fine tension entered her body. The lady also faltered into stillness. That alone would have alerted him to her wakefulness.

He slid his hand across the sheets, the motion evident. Her breath hitched, a sultry sigh— a brush of a butterfly wing whispered over his skin and settled in the room.

She too waited….

Then the lady turned, and he peered down. She stared at him, and something inside his chest cracked open at the sleepy invitation in her gaze. He swallowed back a groan.

I'd be using her.

And that was the bloody truth. He felt knotted with fear and anxiety for his sister and wanted *anything* to distract his mind from visions of her hurting and alone. Burying his cock over and over into a tight welcoming quim would be a heady distraction that would do for the night. And the next night and the next until he found his sister. He recalled Theodosia's provocative defiance that she knew her worth. And that wasn't for him to slake the raw emotions pummeling him into her body. Even if in her eyes he spied a wary kind of desire.

If it was a body he needed to ride for the night, the serving girl had given him several hints earlier that she was available to serve all of his needs. Seb pushed from the bed, grabbing the clothes he set to dry by the grate and headed behind the screen. He dressed with economic motions, leaving off the cravat and the shirt open at the neck. No doubt he looked disreputable, but he still prowled from the room, closing it gently behind him.

"Sebastian."

Theodosia's voice had him pausing in the hallway and turning around. The wall lantern shone over her lovely features and set his heart pounding. She presented a picture that would take any man's breath away. The dark blue night gown clung to her frame, and her heavy mass of golden hair tumbled over her shoulders to settle against her hips. Her figure was sensual and elegant, her ankles dainty and well-turned.

"It is sleeting outside. Do you wish to catch a feverish cold? Are you not afraid you will catch your death to go into the rain once more?"

"I am not going outside."

Her eyes widened, and her lips parted on a silent gasp. She clutched the front of her nightgown and looked beyond his shoulder as if she would see someone there. Even with the distance between them, he saw the understanding dawning on her face.

"Is it necessary?"

That question froze him entirely. And from Theodosia's expression she perfectly understood he was going to find a lady to tup for the night, quieting the fears causing his sleeplessness. Except no arousal filled him at the thought of taking the serving maid to his bed. It was only Theodosia he wanted, no one else. The thought sent a feeling of shock through Seb's body. It hit him then that Theodosia was unlike other women he knew, so different in her manners and candor that he had no comparison.

"Are you offering?" Seb demanded gruffly.

She held his gaze, her eyes huge and heart-stoppingly delicate. Yet there was nothing fragile about this woman. Eyeing him with speechless astonishment, she shook her head and then murmured, "No."

A pity, she was so very lovely and wickedly appealing to his senses. "Then I bid you goodnight, Theodosia. Sleep well. I shall see you in the morning."

Her toes curled onto the carpet. "Good night, Sebastian."

Was that disappointment he heard in her voice?

She melted back into the room and softly closed the door. He slammed his fist into the wall, rattling dust from the ceiling. The hurt burgeoning against his knuckles centered him. Seb leaned against the wall, for God knows how long, unable to take himself downstairs to find the serving woman.

Blowing out a harsh breath, he went back inside the room, shrugged from his jacket, removed his boots, and slid into the bed.

Her uneven breathing suggested she was firmly awake.

"That was quick," she murmured. "Should I have wagered on your prowess I—"

"So help me—" he began to snarl only to stop at the sound of her muffled giggling. How young and sweet she sounded.

"I only tease you, Your Grace."

"I am not a man to be teased."

"Never?"

"Never," he said flatly.

"Without laughter, life has little to no color. I shall be teasing you often, Your Grace."

That soft promise filled him with something warm and unknown instead of irritation. Instead of answering, he remained silent. A rustle sounded, the bed dipped, and she shifted closer. Still far away where he would need to reach an arm's length to touch her.

"I cannot imagine your worry for your sister, and I do not wish to offer empty platitudes and assurances that I cannot guarantee. Please know that I am here should you need a listening ear."

The offer made in that soft voice rocked him. It was the last thing he had expected of her. He turned over Theo's suggestion in his mind, and the way she had said it—only compassion radiated from her tone. As a wealthy duke on the matrimonial market, Seb was long accustomed to ladies employing various wiles designed to ensnare him. Whether it be to become his mistress or his duchess, many had made credible efforts that had grown tiresome even as he vaguely admired their gumption.

Theodosia would not be his bed partner but his friend.

Sebastian's heart stumbled in his chest. He wasn't sure what the feelings were that expanded through his body. They felt heated and pleasant, beating back some of the doubt and fear.

"I also want to assure you that though Perdie is young, she is not impressionable."

A harsh twist went through his heart. "Is that so?

"Yes."

"Eight weeks ago, my sister was blissfully happy, and all she spoke about was getting married. Then she started to visit your 48 Berkeley Square. Do I need to continue?"

"I daresay she wasn't blissfully happy and merely hid it from you."

It leaped inside his chest and clawed at him— guilt and that feeling of helplessness that infuriated him beyond measure. "Fuck!"

He was a man of action and reason. The only thing he needed was a solid plan to find his sister and then deal with the consequences of her action when found. Not to be wallowing in this empty, fucking, useless sensation.

"It would help if you should talk about it," she said softly.

"Talking is not what I want to be doing now."

The raggedness of her breathing suggested she knew exactly what he referred to. *Your move, Theodosia.*

Seb smiled when she scoffed, turned her back to him and muttered, "Good night, Your Grace."

"Good night, Theodosia."

A few beats later, she said, "I do not enjoy traveling for hours in the carriage with little company to keep but my own. I would like a horse ready for me to ride alongside you. I am sure I will find your company congenial. We are partners in finding Perdie, despite your belief that you've coerced me to tag along with you."

CHAPTER TEN

*T*he very next morning, Theo made her way outside to the inn's forecourt, inhaling the crisp spring morning air into her lungs. The duke waited with a handsome chestnut horse, the reins dangling loosely in one of his hands. His earlier uncompromising features were tranquil, his powerful body relaxed atop his stallion, his beautiful blue eyes intent on her. Her mouth dried when his gaze slightly flared, his gloved fingers clenching reflexively on the reins upon noting her riding habit.

He swept off his hat and made his bow to her. "It is a fine morning, Theodosia."

She dipped into a quick curtsey, wanting to curse the fluttering in her stomach. Nay, they were everywhere in her body. Thankfully upon rousing a couple hours ago, she had been alone in the room with only an eager Molly to render assistance.

"It is a perfectly wonderful morning for riding. I fancy I can smell the sea air from here."

The damnable curiosity or awareness should have died away; instead, it had multiplied. The dark green riding habit was one specially made with breeches replacing the pleated skirts. It molded to her figure, leaving little to the imagination. To Theo's mind, it was perfectly freeing and wonderful. She sauntered toward him, nodded gracefully, and went around to the horse.

"What a beauty," she crooned, touching the horse's nose before pushing her foot through the stirrup, grabbing the pommel, and hauling herself with perfect ease onto the saddle without calling for the mounting blocks.

She cast him a sidelong glance and tossed her head. "What men can do…women can do."

Sebastian turned away, but she spied the barely-there smile before it vanished from her sight.

"I've sent the carriages ahead. I hope to reach Brighton by noon," he said, turning his horse down the driveway, turning him into a trot.

Theo followed suit, easily keeping pace with the duke. Tension radiated from his frame, the hands gripping the reins were stiff, his top hat shadowing his face so Theo could not even hazard a guess as to what he might be feeling.

"Your Grace…" Theo began, only to stop when he looked at her.

The duke might be silent, but his eyes shone

with his private agony. Last night he had been a scoundrel, and she'd done her best to sleep without thinking of how close he slept or what he wanted from her. He hadn't taken up her offer to speak, and she had thought this morning of any way she could relieve his worry. A part of her questioned why she was so concerned about a man she hardly knew, but it was also against her nature to see someone's worry and ignore their distress.

The gentle breeze lifted the tendrils of hair from her forehead. "I know you are very worried about Perdie, Sebastian," she murmured.

The duke did not reply but remained silent. Theo could not take offense, unable to imagine the fear he and his mother must currently endure.

He drew his horse to a halt suddenly. "Rakes are notorious for preying on young, inexperienced girls."

Theo slowed her mount to a stop. "Is that what you've been thinking? That a bounder has seduced Perdie into running away?"

Piercing blue eyes swung back to her. "It is a possibility."

"If I might put forth an opinion, Your Grace, I do not believe your sister to be a lady of such easy persuasion. She loves Lord Owen very much and was quite pained in imagining a life without him. If she had another admirer, I would be most surprised."

A frown split the duke's brow. "Would you have

believed her capable of running away from home?"

"No."

"Then how can you trust anything she has ever told you in the past?"

From the low throb in his voice, she understood then how much Perdie's actions had hurt their brotherly and sisterly bond. The duke possibly now distrusted every moment that had passed between himself and Perdie. A sadness pierced Theo's heart. "I believe your sister felt trapped…"

A tic jerked in his jaw. "Trapped? She got everything she has ever asked for! Even when I thought her too young to be engaged, she cried and pled for weeks until I relented and agreed to the betrothal. And perhaps that was my grave mistake. I indulged and spoilt her, and she has repaid that love and care to her family with selfish disregard of how they might worry. She also disregarded any thoughts for her reputation and her family's position within society." Urging his mount forward, he calmly said, "Forgive my outburst. It is nonsensical to speak of what could have been done differently."

Theo was almost impressed how easily he controlled that raw burst of emotion, smoothing his face into a mask of implacable politeness. They trotted for a few more paces, and she noted the tension still held his shoulders rigid. The imagination could be a cruel thing indeed, and as older protective brothers were wont to do, he would not think that she was safe and happy somewhere. It was easier to imagine the worse, facing the horror of it to prepare oneself.

"Your Grace…Sebastian…"

He slowed his horse, glancing at her at the intimate use of his name.

"Would you like to race?"

He stared at her, clearly surprised. Of course, she wouldn't tell him she wanted to save his mind from the worry he was endured.

"Race you?"

"Yes."

"I am an incomparable rider, Theodosia. You've already lost."

She scoffed. "Your arrogance truly knows no bounds."

"I supposed not," he replied with a small curve to his mouth.

"Do you see those wildflowers in the distance and that rather large rock? See you there!" Theo said, nudging her horse into a flat-out run. A quick glance behind her showed that the duke had taken up her challenge. Delight rushed through her body, and her heartbeat quickened as they sped past the rolling countryside—a blur of greens and the bright splash of flowers. The steady sounds of hoofbeats thumping the ground in a thrilling rhythm urged her to encourage her horse to move faster. They raced neck to neck for a few minutes, the wind whipping at her face, the power of the horse jarring her in a few places, and the sheer joy of being free surging through her heart.

They came to a shuddering halt, and Theo laughed, tipping her head to the sky. "Now wasn't that glorious?"

A smile lingered about his mouth. "I daresay it was. You are also an incomparable rider."

She regarded him in mock astonishment. "Was that a compliment?"

"I've been known to give them," he said drily.

"Thank you, Your Grace. I do like being flattered."

Whatever she said appealed to his sense of humor, for his mouth softened, and a glint of amusement entered his eyes. "I would like to tell you something else about your sister," Theo murmured. "And I hope the knowledge might ease some of the worry in your heart, if not the pain of her decision."

There was a moment of tense silence. Then the duke said, "Tell me."

"You are very much larger than I am, but I was able to drop you on your arse," she said with a smile. "Perdie has that same skill."

A swift intake of breath and his gaze sharpened. "She does?"

"Yes. We do not meet at 48 Berkeley Square to gossip. Well, not only to gossip," Theo said with a light laugh. "Perdie is very well able to defend herself from rakes and ruffians should the need arise. She also knows how to fence. Her level has not reached mastery, but she is good. She also knows the art of boxing, and I believe a facer from her would leave many with sore feelings of pride and a hurting cheek."

"My sister learned all this from your…ladies club?"

"Yes."

"And all the other ladies learned as well?"

"Once they are interested. It is not mandatory."

"And what else besides fighting, wagers, and dares does your club offer?"

"Fencing, boxing, we read all sorts of books gentlemen believe us too gentle to read," Theo said teasingly. "Most importantly, we have friendship… and we support each other in our endeavors no matter how outlandish it might seem. A dream is a dream."

The duke fell silent, and they trotted in that companionable atmosphere, and Theo hoped he could rest a bit easier knowing she was not the helpless damsel he imagined.

"You are a very interesting woman, Lady Theodosia."

"So, you've said, Sebastian," Theo replied with a tip of her feathered hat.

He chuckled, and it transformed him entirely— the duke was simply too appealing. A hot feeling pierced her belly, and she had to look away from his countenance.

"Thank you for letting me know about Perdie's skills. I do feel better for knowing it."

"You are welcome," she said, smiling at him.

"Why precisely did you open this club of yours?"

She jolted, truly surprised at the question.

"I told you…I find you interesting," the duke said, his gaze skipping over her face with intimate slowness.

"I…" Theo glanced away for a brief moment. It has been so long since she had genuine discourse with a gentleman where she had to reveal something private about herself. The light flirtations with gentlemen of society held little substance, and what friendship she owned were all with the ladies of her club. "I have no notion where to start, so perhaps it is best I do not start at all."

The duke raised a brow. "We have a few hours ahead of us before we reach Brighton."

Theo bit into her lower lip.

"My question made you nervous."

"I…" she exhaled gustily. "I am not used to speaking candidly with a gentleman."

"I quite like the idea of being your first."

She searched his expression to see if he teased, and she only saw curious fascination. "I was married off very young, and my husband was much older than I am."

"I recall the many mentions in the scandal sheets. I believe you were eighteen."

"Seventeen." Theo rolled her eyes in an unladylike fashion. "Yes, our match was mocked, and I was even referred to by some as notorious and compared to a flytrap." And even to this season, some whispered behind their fans whenever she entered a ballroom. "Our marriage was…unusual."

"How so?"

"That, Your Grace, I cannot own to in any serious detail. You must simply accept it was unusual, and within its confines, I was unhappy and lonely. It was only in my dreams I could see the possibilities of the life I hungered to live."

His expression grew thoughtful. "And what did you hunger for?"

"I suppose the freedom to laugh."

He visibly jolted. "Laughter?"

"Sounds ridiculous, doesn't it? I could not show the world how unhappy or frightened I was to have married a man older than my father, else I would be ungrateful. Viscount Winfern saved my father from debtor prison and our entire family from scandal. How could I show that I was terribly uncertain of marriage and my new role in the world?"

Theo tipped her face to the sky, lost in the memories for several moments. "My mother and father happily went on to reside in Venice with the money made through my union. My brother lives in Hampshire with his wife and two children, quite happy he had not been required to marry someone he does not love to save the family from penury. It is odd, but I did not laugh for months after my marriage. I did not realize it until I was at a garden party hosted by Lady Pettigrew, and a flock of geese attacked Countess Merriweather's hat and three other young ladies. It was as if a dam had been released. I laughed. We were shushed, and I was even reminded how unflattering it was for a viscountess to laugh so raucously. I showed my teeth!"

Theo chuckled at the ridiculous memory that was such a pivotal moment in her life. "We four ladies ran toward the lake, and once we were from earshot, we laughed as loudly as we could and for as long as we wanted. It felt…freeing, and it was then I realized I had not laughed in months. I found a friendship with those ladies that day, which is more than I could ever hope for. Their love and friendship saved me from many lonely nights and through so many doubts and fears. I was incredibly naïve when I married, and I was not alone in this. Many young girls in our society marry at seventeen. Many have children by twenty. And many of us are no longer laughing…that is if we were ever allowed to laugh a little because we must not be improper, you know."

A breeze stirred the air, carrying the scent of spring, and she inhaled it deep into her lungs. "Many gentlemen believe ladies are dull-witted and inarticulate. I daresay it soothes their vanity to think such nonsense. Ladies are groomed by their mothers and governesses to be biddable, hiding their natural wit and grace. Such *nonsense*. At my home…at my home, they are free to blunder without a sharp reprimand or a scandal ruining their chances. They are also free to shine as brightly as they can without fear of being rebuked. Many young ladies let life happen to them…and they are not a part of it, never truly living for themselves."

"You hope to offer them that?"

She laughed a bit self-consciously. "It sounds a bit silly perhaps, but I do hope that being at my club, they might find a slice of joy and comfort I did in my friendships and freedom to live a little."

"It is not silly…but selfless and admirable."

She had not expected that praise, knowing he found her to be ineligible company for his sister. "I do believe how I view life might influence the ladies that visit my home to rebel more against dictates that stifle them, to dare to live their lives independently," Theo said softly, unable to hide from the role she played in Perdie's actions.

"Perhaps it is better to have a sister who would fight against a fate that would make her unhappy instead of one who is biddable, swallow the bitterness in her heart, and endure a life of unhappiness." His voice was flat and cold, uninviting more discourse.

Several moments passed in silence and she stole a glance at the duke. And so easily she lost her ability to breathe. The duke was gazing steadily at

LOVE ME, IF YOU DARE

her. Sebastian stared at her with an expression of such naked longing, her gloved fingers as they twisted the reins shook. "Sebastian…I…were you staring at me this entire time?"

"Yes. You are not to blame yourself for Perdie's action."

"Have you not charged me as responsible?"

"If my sister trusted me, she would have confided her fears. No one is responsible for that but Perdie and myself. I cannot believe you've had other members act with such disregard for their reputation and families."

Theo blinked. Last week she had at least five other ladies drink a bottle of their finest brandy and dare each other with many scandalous taunts. Some so wicked, reputations would be ruined should they ever dared to be so naughty.

"I can tell from your expression that I am off the mark," he said, "I am intrigued."

It felt as if an invisible thread had been woven between them, and now it tugged, pulling her a bit closer to him. Theo couldn't explain the ease at which she conversed with the man. That in itself felt freeing…and also a comfort.

She made a non-committal sound. "As you are not a member at 48 Berkeley Square, I cannot divulge it."

"Thank you for telling me about your club," he said, the touch of his eyes never leaving her face.

What do you search for, Sebastian?

Yet she did not boldly ask but kept her gaze averted, afraid he would see the answering want inside her gaze.

"Tell me, Theodosia, was your curiosity satisfied?"

She shifted her regard back to his, startled by the question. A deep awareness filled the air around them, encompassing throughout her body. She had a fleeting recollection of this very feeling last night when she had stared up at him sleepily. "Yes…it was." A misdirection she hoped he would not see through.

The duke did not reply, but his mouth curved, and that smile held a wicked kind of knowledge.

"Do I want to know what you are thinking about?"

"No."

Theo did not understand why the very thought of wanting the duke scared her so. But it did. The idea of wanting him must never be given any serious consideration. But no amount of sensible reasoning stopped the warmth fluttering low in her belly and spreading throughout her body. Something impish rose inside of her. "I dare you…"

He sent her a sharp glance of surprise. "What?"

"I dare you to tell me…"

"Your sensibilities would be alarmed."

"Now I am even more curious. Do you accept my dare?" *Theo, stop; you are teasing a predator.*

CHAPTER ELEVEN

I dare you...

The smile Theodosia sent his way was full of captivating vivacity, and there lingered a dangerous sparkle in her eyes. This little lady liked living on the edge, even if she did not admit to it. Of course, Sebastian would not dare tell her the carnal thoughts and odd yearnings she roused in his heart. Such confessions had no place between them unless she was willing to become his mistress. The very idea that she would be amenable to such an arrangement had heat stirring in his loins.

Bloody hell. He was really becoming muddled.

At his continued silence, Theodosia made an awful squawking sound, and Sebastian grinned. "The chicken really is not a coward, you know. I recall visiting one of my tenant farmers with my father. I was a lad of twelve, and a chicken, a hen I believed, chased me for miles. I had nightmares for weeks about that damn hen."

Theodosia laughed, the sound light and lovely, and it caught at something tender inside Sebastian. For so long she had lacked laughter, a thing he could not imagine. Even through his family's most painful experience, his father's death, they had supported each other with love and recollecting of memories that had brought laughter and tears. Without laughter, there must have been sadness, perhaps pain, and undoubtedly loneliness. She would have endured this without the support of those close to her, with her parents living lavishly abroad and her brother contentedly in the countryside.

She had been used and discarded, and not only by the man she'd married.

"I supposed you were mortally embarrassed to be fleeing from a hen!" she said with a chortle that shook her shoulders. "I cannot imagine it! You are so very proper and duke like...I cannot see you running from a chicken, your face filled with fright."

If only she knew how improper he could be. "I admit it took me a few days before I could look my father in the eye."

"When you did, what did he say."

"Ah, it was a confession. That particular hen was cantankerous and had even chased my father the day before. He praised my swift thinking in retreating from a battle I would surely lose."

He really liked her laughter.

Theodosia stared at him, her expression suddenly contemplative. "I can tell that you miss him."

He trotted a little closer, staying in her line of vision. "He was a good father, husband, and duke. His family loved him, and so did his staff and tenants. I found myself wondering what he would have done to find Perdie. Though she barely recalls it, father doted on her."

Theo wondered if there had been a time her father doted on her. She doubted it, truly cannot recall ever having his approval or affection. It occurred to her she did not long to see her mother or father. "What exactly are you doing to find Perdie?"

"My plan is to visit all the places Perdie is familiar with. I am hoping she will seek comfort and refuge in places she knows. We will start with all the houses that belong to the family."

"Are there a lot of places?"

"Nine spread throughout England, Scotland, and a chateau in France and a villa in Italy. Given that the countries are still stabilizing after Napoleon's war, I do not think she would dare travel to France or anywhere abroad."

"Have you sent the hired runners to all of your homes?"

"I have. Though I trust they will do a credible job, I cannot leave it all to them while I sit idly waiting for news."

"I understand."

They rode in silence for several minutes, and Sebastian appreciated she wasn't a lady given to nervous chattering. Her eyes were bright with humor or perhaps just the joy of living—the earlier echoes of emptiness gone. They picked up their pace, riding across the country roads to Brighton. The quiet between them felt companionable and pleasant.

Why do I find you so appealing? He silently wondered.

The only things that should be consuming his thoughts now were Perdie—finding her, then mending everything that had been broken. Theodosia had his gut in knots and not in a flattering way.

Upon arriving in Brighton Sebastian immediately directed them to the house he owned. Perdie had fallen in love with the seaside, and each year he had taken her and his mother for a trip. A thorough but discreet search revealed Perdie was not in Brighton. The hope he'd been holding close now sat like a heavy boulder on Sebastian's shoulders. For over an hour, he walked trying to work through the cold knot of doubt growing inside. Sebastian found himself by the seaside, staring out into the ocean and the lapping waves.

Thankfully, the beach was empty of sea bathers, for the sun was lowering in the sky, and the visitors to the area would flock to the town's entertainments.

"Where are you, Perdie?"

He thought of all the places they'd visited together over the years, all the places she loved. Dipping into his pocket, he withdrew the crumpled letter and read it once more.

Did someone take you, perhaps forced you to write this?

He immediately dismissed the desperate thoughts. No villain would have taken a lady's maid and a companion too. Perdie had planned this. Each time he thought of it, Seb felt a shock of disbelief in his body, still unable to comprehend his sister would act in such a foolhardy manner. They had always been close. Always. He couldn't imagine what Perdie believed she had to keep secret.

Finding herself. What the hell did that mean? And what if he should heed her plea to leave her be. Could he really act according to her wishes? The denial that roared through him then was fierce and uncompromising. Leaving his sister alone in the world was not a thought to be borne.

The soft padding of a footstep drifted closer, but it was Theodosia's scent of jasmine and something elusive that raked at his senses. Seb turned, watching as Theodosia made her way to him. Oddly, that hard twist in his gut loosened and another unknown but quite pleasant sensation drifted through him. She came up to him, looking exquisitely lovely. She wore her hair in a loose braid without a bonnet atop her head. Her dress was a simple blue high waist gown that clung alluringly to her frame.

"Perdie is not here in Brighton," Theodosia murmured.

"She isn't."

They turned to the sea, staring at the frothy waves in silence. Seb acknowledged her presence at the moment felt comforting.

"My father took me here some years ago for the grand opening of the Theatre Royal. I believe it was in 1807. They played Hamlet that night, and I still recall how great it was sitting amongst the crowd and being a part of that energy. The feeling of being a part of something magical, the majesty of the actors on stage, the sheer presence of Charles Kemble."

A smile tipped the corner of her mouth. "I saw him once at Drury Lane. He was quite magnificent."

"Very much like our Prince Regent, my father loved the arts and took me to many plays. The first time I shared that story with Perdie, she wanted to visit Brighton and see Hamlet for herself at the same theatre. She wanted to promenade down the Steyne—to walk in a place our father had been, to sit in a place where he had sat, to laugh and enjoy life as once he had. Somehow, I thought it one of the places she always felt connected to the man she mostly knew through my stories of our time together here."

Theodosia faced him, her eyes bright with sympathy. "I wish so very much I knew where she was." She lifted a hand as if to touch his face but lowered it back to her side. "How do we find her?" That question was a mere whisper of sound.

A hard determination filled his heart. "I'll keep searching. We leave Brighton at the crack of dawn. I've already stationed trusted men here to be on the lookout. If they see her, a message will be sent to my man of affairs in London and the Duchess in Maidstone. They will know where to find me."

"Isn't there somewhere special to Perdie, more so than others? You have several homes, and you both seemed to travel regularly; they all cannot be equal."

Seb lifted his head to the sky, thinking. "Our father died when Perdie was only eight years old. Each year I took her to the places my father took me as a lad. He did so mostly to show me what my future responsibilities entailed. But also for me to learn the land and the people. But when I showed each place to Perdie, it was a way for her to connect with our father, to know him, and to also broaden her horizon." Without looking at her, he said, "I can feel you staring, Theodosia."

She glanced away, but he could see that her cheeks were flushed with color. "I—"

An awareness slammed into him. "The cottage."

Seb closed his eyes briefly, thinking of the possibility of her being there.

"What cottage?"

"Our grandmother left us a cottage in Kent. It is not a part of the dukedom holdings, and it is not as stately. Only twelve rooms staffed by a housekeeper, a scullery maid, a cook, and a footman. We have not been there in almost four years if I recollect it correctly." *Bloody hell*. Why had he not thought of the cottage sooner. "I've not sent any runners there. Perdie loved visiting the cottage."

"Then we journey to the cottage tomorrow," Theodosia said without any perceptible hesitation.

Seb stared at her, admiring her uncomplaining nature. Under the gentle glow of the moonlight, she appeared so very lovely. He had not treated her too kindly or in a gentleman-like fashion, ordering her from the comfort of her home to gallivant with him across England searching for his wayward sister. He had driven them at a hard pace, and she had not complained. Her backside might be sore, though she had sat in the saddle with the grace and agility of an extremely skilled rider.

Theodosia did not complain. She was indeed made of stern stuff. "Thank you, Theodosia, for accompanying me."

She made no quip about being kidnapped but smiled. "It is my pleasure, Sebastian." Theodosia turned away and started to walk back toward the general direction of his house. A peculiar feeling rose inside of him, and he acknowledged he would miss her presence. A part of him was tempted to ask her to stay, but he gritted his teeth and suppressed the urgings. She paused, and his heart jolted.

She slowly faced him. "Will you join me for dinner? When I left your house, your cook was preparing a most sumptuous dinner. I recall something about scallops in garlic butter sauce, braised duck, and fish."

Sebastian didn't think it wise to dine with her, not when his thoughts about her were so muddled. It felt like she happened in his life at the wrong moment. "No."

"You have not eaten since we left the inn early this morning."

"I need to clear my thoughts."

"You mean to promenade along the Steyne? Do you need company?"

"I will contrive to keep myself tolerably engaged, and I mean to swim."

Her eyes widened, and she glanced toward the waves that danced and crashed against gravel and rocks. "The water must be frightfully cold, and it looks rough."

"It will do perfectly."

"What will it do other than cause a feverish cold?"

"I am made of sturdy stuff."

She sniffed delicately. "Why do you wish to swim in this terribly cold water?"

"I need the distraction," he admitted.

"From?"

Thoughts of you…Perdie…everything. Instead of saying those things, Sebastian murmured, "Good night, Theodosia."

She stared at him, and he was unable to decipher the intent in her gaze. Finally, she nodded and turned away. The breath he'd been holding slowly escaped, and he tugged at his cravat, loosening the intricate knots.

"Sebastian?"

Theodosia walked toward him, almost hurrying in her haste. Looking behind her, he saw no threat. He took a step toward her. "What is it?" he asked, a sense of urgency beating inside him.

Her eyes were wide, and in her golden-brown depths, he spied fright, vulnerability, and perhaps…desire?"

"Theodosia I—"

"Let me be your distraction…if only for a moment," she said, her chest lifting on a rapid breath.

He must have misunderstood. "What?"

"We can dance under the stars…"

"The sky is overcast."

Her lips trembled, and he saw it was because she suppressed laughter.

"We can talk, keep each other company, the most perfect distractions from unwanted thoughts, wouldn't you agree?"

"The air is becoming chilled."

She stepped closer to him, and his heart almost jumped from his chest. "Theo—"

"Or we can do this…"

And to Sebastian's shock, she leaned into his body, tipped onto her booted toes, and pressed her mouth perfectly against his.

CHAPTER TWELVE

*W*hat the devil had possessed her? A thrill skittered through Theodosia, terrifying and exhilarating. *I am kissing Sebastian.* If she fell for this man, when their journey ended, as it inevitably would, her heart would shatter. Theo sensed it with every part of her being. Yet she did not pull away from the devastating pleasure of being in his arms, of being kissed senseless. No, she pressed even closer to him, taunting him to kiss her deeper with small glides of her tongue and little nips against his lips when they broke apart.

Theo stepped back from the precipice of recklessness she'd just hurled herself toward. Or she tried to. The duke's hands were clamped firmly on her hips, holding her close to his body. His eyes glittered in the dark, and the half-moon cast his face in shadows of harsh, almost frightening carnality. His breathing was harsh, and Theo could feel the tension inside his body. "I…I do not know why I did that," she murmured against his mouth.

"Liar," he said, just as softly and even a bit affectionately. "You have been wanting to kiss me again since we last tested our curiosity. I know for the taste of you has been stamped into my very bones."

The words burned themselves inside her. It felt good being with the duke. He made her feel alive. A startling notion for whatever connection they had would not last beyond finding Perdie. Alive…a very odd awareness, to be sure, but it was only now Theo realized how many desires she had suppressed. Now they slowly stirred, leaping to life with mere conversations, a fleeting touch, a longing look.

He did a lot of that—gazing at her. She found it somewhat disconcerting but also wonderful because that intent stare made her feel beautiful. *I must not fall in love with you…that way, I'll be able to bear it when we part, and all this will be a wonderful memory.* It was unimaginable to have this awareness darting through her, so much so she willingly danced close to the duke's fire.

"Admit it," he coaxed, still holding her scandalously close to his body.

"Yes, when you kissed me, I hated that a few hours later I lost the taste of you." It was a mere murmur of sound from her lips, but he had faltered into remarkable stillness. But not his heart, that beat a furious rhythm against her body.

"I kissed you now because I wanted to remove the shadows from your eyes and replace it with something else. I did not want you to go into the night and the waters with torment and doubt chasing you."

"So, you wanted to replace my worry with a hunger that fucking torments me?"

She jerked at the sensual crudity, quite aware of the blush engulfing her body. "Is it not a better torment?"

"One will not do."

Her heart started to beat faster, and though she knew what he implied, Theo still asked, "One will not do?"

He dragged her up against his body, almost violently, and with a gasp, she clasped his shoulders. The sensation that she'd roused a sleeping tiger invaded her senses. She drew a silent breath and held it for a few moments before releasing it slowly.

"One taste of you will *not* do," he said against the corner of her mouth.

A startling warmth invaded her, and the shock sent prickles all over her body. A swell of yearning went through her heart, and Theo feared it was reflected in her gaze as she stared up at him. The harsh sensuality of his features softened, yet somehow became more carnal...more tempting. A terrible weak-kneed feeling assailed Theo.

"Open for me," he said.

Theo gave Sebastian her mouth and he consumed her. With a muffled moan of pleasure, she rose onto the tip of her toes, sinking the front of her boots deep into the wet pebbles. She twined her arms around his neck, returning his kiss with fiery passion. Heat spiraled through Theo with each tangle of their tongues, with each wordless murmur and impatient yet desperately needy sighs. His mouth teased, but it also ravished, leaving her mouth bruised. He promised such pleasure, but she sensed should they ever make love, he would not always be a tender lover.

An answering hunger rose inside her when he cupped her buttocks and dragged her even further up, so she felt the proof of his arousal. The waves crashed around them, and she distantly felt the cold water lapping at her half-boots and dress. As the sensations almost overwhelmed her, Sebastian's mouth grew gentle, his kisses turning coaxing and seductive, drawing Theo deeper into a world of feeling and need.

Their kiss broke, and she made a soft sound of protest at the loss of his lips against her. The cool breeze rushing over the surface of the sea to violently whip at her dress brought Theo firmly to her senses. She stepped back, though it was very hard to do so being engulfed by such want. Theo touched the corner of his mouth, absurdly pleased to see his lips were also swollen. "Dream a little of… me tonight and worry less."

Then she turned and walked away, shatteringly aware of his piercing gaze upon her back.

I dared a little…and God help me, but I want to dare so much more.

AFTER TRAVELING for two days with little rest in between, Theo and the Duke arrived in Dunston, a small, picturesque village nestled in the southern part of Kent. They canted through the village square and were treated to openly curious stares by the villagers.

They dismounted, leading their horses by the reins. Several people recognized him and offered greetings which he returned. He even exchanged a few words with the vicar's wife, Mrs. Bryant, who had appeared fit to burst at the seams from that delight. He also spoke briefly with the squire's wife, Mrs. Adams, a vision of fashionable elegance traveling with two maids who helped her hand out food baskets to some of the villagers. Almost everyone ogled Theo, and Sebastian introduced her to Mrs. Bryant and Mrs. Adams as a friend. Even being a widow, it was dreadfully improper traveling alone with the duke like this. And perhaps it was for that very reason, Theo found herself enjoying being with him, even with the gravity of the matter before them and the judgmental manner in which the squire's wife had stared.

"Elise has missed you quite dreadfully, Your Grace," Mrs. Adams said, smiling prettily up at the duke.

Theo was glad for the veil which covered her face, for she glared at the lady and the way she swayed toward the duke, delicately resting her hand on his arm. Jealousy spurred through Theo, and she sucked in a soft breath before she grinned. How ridiculous she was!

"I have missed Elise as well. I do hope she will call upon me soon."

Mrs. Adams beamed at the duke as if he had just handed her a chest of rubies. A loud bark sounded, and a large shaggy dog loped across the lawns in great leaps and set its front paws up against his legs.

"Horatio," the duke said, laughing as he stooped to scratch behind the dog's ears. "How I've missed you."

The dog let out a series of high wines and barks, clearly just as pleased to see his friend. A young girl of about twelve hurried over and squealed her happiness when she saw the duke. She hurtled herself at him, and he enfolded her into a hug. Mrs. Adams cleared her throat, and the little girl flushed before drawing back and dipping into a most elegant curtsy.

Theo was charmed. The duke stood and returned her bow with exaggerated civility and charm. The young girl giggled before turning curious eyes to Theo. Introductions were made, pleasantries exchanged, and promises extracted that they would be at tonight's village fair. A May Day spring celebration.

They had both promised it before remounting and trotting away.

"You were Horatio's master once?" the dog had seemed very sad to see the duke leaving.

"I was. We both saved Elise the last time I was here from drowning. She had nightmares after, and the only thing that soothed her was his presence."

Theo recalled the love she'd seen on the duke's face just now when he greeted his dog.

"It must have been painful to part from him."

"She needed him more than I did, and he was quite happy to stay with her." That guarded look once more entered the duke's eyes. "Perdie is not here," he said slowly and distinctively.

Sudden awareness filled Theo. The anxiousness of hoping was the reason he'd stopped. "You are thinking if she was here…"

"Mrs. Adams would surely have mentioned it."

"We cannot know the full of it until we reach the cottage." Perhaps Perdie was there and was being very discreet. Theo doubted it, and the heaviness inside her grew. She prayed he would find his sister at the cottage. England was so vast. Though the duke was undoubtedly wealthy and had the resources to hire many people to aid him, his sister could be irrevocably lost to him and his mother.

They rode in silence for several more minutes until a large house loomed in the distance. It was surrounded by a park wall and miles of rolling lawns and forestry.

The 'cottage' was a charming manor situated on a small hill overlooking the village. Once they reached the forecourt, they dismounted and handed their reins to a waiting groom. Sebastian made his way inside, and Theo hurried to keep up with his long strides.

The housekeeper greeted him with surprised gladness, dipping into a deep curtsy. She was very pretty and a plump woman of uncertain age. She wore a lace cap, and soft red hair curled along her nape and at her forehead.

"Mrs. Thomas is Lady Perdita here?" the duke asked abruptly, walking down the hallway and into a large room which revealed itself to be a tastefully furnished drawing-room.

The housekeeper flushed and hurried to speech, "A few days ago she was here, Your Grace, but she departed the very next day."

Theo gasped. Why would Perdie leave so soon?

Sebastian scrubbed a hand over his face with a hand that visibly trembled. "Was she hurt?" he demanded gruffly.

"Your Grace," the startled housekeeper cried. "*Nay*! Milady was as fit as a fiddle."

"Was there anything that aroused suspicion in your mind? Anything that made you feel worried for her?"

Mrs. Thomas shook her head most vigorously. "I merely thought it unseemly Lady Perdie traveled with only that companion and a lady maid. I saw no footmen or coachmen in your livery, Your Grace. And she left something for you."

She bustled away and returned a few moments later, a letter in her hand. "Lady Perdie directed me to hand you this letter should you come here, or to mail it to you in London after a week has passed."

Sebastian took it, and it was clear Mrs. Thomas wanted to know what was happening but dared not ask in fear of overstepping. She bobbed a curtsy and withdrew. At the door she paused, and turned around, looking quite anxious. "There was something else, Your Grace."

"Tell me."

"Lady Perdie walked with a bow and arrows and also a fencing sword."

This was received with evident incredulity. "A bow and arrows?"

"Yes, Your Grace. I thought she might have wanted to practice her arrows, so I instructed Jarvis to set up straws targets thirty feet apart on the eastern section of the lawns."

"Thank you, Mrs. Thomas."

She bobbed and hurried from the room.

Sebastian stared at the letter, his expression

carefully guarded. Theo suspected he was knotted inside, so she silently padded away to afford him privacy. She would find the housekeeper and introduce herself.

"Stay."

That soft command arrested her movements. Theo turned around. He had not lifted his regard from the letter but had been aware of her every movement. Sebastian opened the letter, but he did not read it, handing it to Theo. She took it, watching him carefully. He walked over to the window and braced an elbow on the pane, staring out into the forestry.

Theo walked over to him and started to read,

Dearest Sebastian,

I intended to stay at Rosemead cottage, but then I realized that you would surely come to find me here. I am not ready to return home. I promise to do so in time for Lady Michaels' midnight ball in June. Forgive me the worry I have caused you and mama, but I must do this.

Your sister,

Perdie.

She had anticipated him going there and sought to reassure him. Theo folded the letter and drifted closer to the duke. "I believe as reckless and silly as Perdie is, she is very much safe for now."

The tension leaked from his shoulders, and he lowered his elbow from the window. The duke faced her. She fought the urge to fidget under his unwavering regard.

"She has promised to return home in a few weeks."

"Yes."

The sardonic curl to his mouth became more pronounced. "She expects me to trust her alone for that long."

This was perhaps not the wisest thing to say, but Theo murmured, "What men have done...ladies can most certainly do."

Astonishment lit in his eyes before they shuttered. He leaned close—close enough to breathe deeply of her, which shockingly he did.

"Then what do you suggest I do. Sit idly and simply hope my sister will not fall prey to a villain."

"Not to sit idly or to sit in fear. But perhaps accept that Perdie is determined to have a few days to herself."

"Don't you mean weeks? Lady Michaels' ball is almost a month away."

"She is not hapless. Perdie is a witty, smart, and capable young lady. We can continue searching... but you need a break from the intense pressure you've placed yourself under these past few days. That break would come if you chose to trust in her just a little bit."

His eyes darkened, and he made a sound of incredulity. "Why the hell do you care about the pressures I've endured."

She lifted a shoulder in an inelegant shrug, quite aware of the pounding in her heart. "I just do."

They stared at each other, and though it was tempting to look away, she held the fierceness of his stare.

"And how do you suggest I pass the time?" he drawled, almost mockingly.

"Attend a village festival with me."

He blinked, and she almost smiled. "The annual festival?"

"Yes. Drink, dance, and make merry. At least for one night, and then tomorrow…"

"Tomorrow, I continue searching."

"Yes."

A wry smile twisted his mouth. "I have the oddest feeling if I do not slow down and see you…I might regret it."

That soft, almost befuddled confession robbed her of air. Theo did not comment on it; instead, she said, "So I shall see you tonight in the village then."

He dipped and brushed his lips over hers. "How curious are you now, Theodosia?"

Her entire body went hot. She allowed her gaze to linger on his lush mouth.

He shot her a brief, unreadable look, then the devil murmured, "I can tell you are."

The memory of their kiss had woven itself into her dreams. Each day within his company felt like an exercise in restraint. She worked to keep their conversation casual. Theo did not believe she would maintain a friendship with a duke. That would be flying too high. Except his kisses lingered too deep within her. Theo tried to persuade herself it meant nothing. People, though they pretended the opposite, stole kisses with each other quite frequently. To kiss a handsome man was entirely normal. To have liked it was also normal. To think about it, *very* normal.

She took a deep breath. *Please let this all be normal.* Or she was in for a fine disappointment if she dared to hold any silly girlish fantasies about the duke. She stared at that taunting glint in his gaze. *Do I really dare…to do more than kiss you?* Theo could hardly describe the warm feeling hugging her body. She tipped onto her toe so she could press her mouth close to his ear. "You are laboring under a delusion. I am not even a smidgen curious."

Then she withdrew, whirled, and walked away, smiling because the blasted man behind her was chuckling in rich anticipation.

CHAPTER THIRTEEN

*A*n hour after eating a light repast with the duke, Theo clambered up the winding staircase behind him. Despite the largeness of the duke's country cottage there was a feeling of comfort, of the space being a home instead of a house. The large windows on all the floors were framed by sweeping curtains in yellow and crème silk brocade. The duke stopped at a door, pushed it opened and waved his hand for her to enter.

"Oh, how lovely!" she said, glancing around the large room.

"This will be your room."

She slanted him a quick, searching glance. "My own room?"

"Yes."

It was a splendid room, with elegant furniture in Italian marble and carved mahogany and a soft carpet. The four-poster bed with its draped pale blue damask curtains, tied back to the posts with tasseled ropes, seemed to dominate the room. Thick carpet patterned in shades of blue complementing the curtains covered the floor, and the lower half of the walls had been paneled in rich, dark wood. "I am surprised I am finally given the privilege."

"You flatter me with the regret I hear in your tone," he said drily. "Had I known you wanted to keep sleeping with me, I would have made arrangements. It is not too late to oblige you."

Theo glanced up at him through her lashes and flashed him a taunting smile. "What you hear is delight in knowing I will be able to sleep in the nude at last."

Rendered almost inarticulate by that retort, he groaned and dragged a hand through his black hair. "That is an image I could have done without as I try to sleep tonight," he said with a black scowl. "I will congratulate myself later for my restraint."

Theo laughed when he bowed and quickly made his way from her room. It was fun teasing the duke. Theo was determined to have fun at the village fair in a few hours, and she was even more determined not to allow Sebastian to linger too much in the torment of worrying over his sister's safety. His honor, and his love for Lady Perdita would not allow him to stop searching, and Theo did not think he should. Not with so much on the line if a scoundrel should discover an heiress like Perdie traveled alone. Though Theo had that worry, she also trusted in Perdie's abilities to defend herself and also in her cleverness.

With the aid of Molly, she undressed and indulged in a hot, relaxing bath. Wrapped in a large towel, she fell asleep on the bed, only to jolt awake yawning. A quick glance at the clock revealed she had slept for almost four hours. Theo hurriedly dressed in a simple but fashionable gown, coaxing Molly to style her hair in a simple chignon. Theo hurried downstairs with some eagerness. She went outside and encountered the housekeeper returning with a basket of freshly picked hothouse tomatoes.

Theo did not call for a horse but hurried along the lane toward the village square. She was a great observer of life. She noted that anticipation ran high amongst the villagers for the upcoming festivities. The loveliest part of the village square was the arched stone bridge which was situated above a gurgling river which continued downhill. Several couples stood on that bridge with the overhanging boughs of weeping willow trees, tossing stones and coins into the water, making whimsical wishes.

SHE MINGLED and chatted for a few minutes with the vicar's wife and the vicar himself. Theo learned that the villagers were very proud that the duke formerly favored them with a visit at least once per year and was saddened they had not seen them in almost four years. Theo encountered Mrs. Adams, who stared at Theo's uncovered face with little effort to hide her inquisitiveness.

"The villagers are curious about you," Mrs. Adams said with a nosy laugh. "Of course, they know any guest of the duke is assumed to be the most distinguished company."

Theo was saved the necessity of a reply by Sebastian's arrival. His blue superfine jacket was immaculately tailored. His fawn-colored trousers were fitted to his frame in a manner that suggested they had been tailored by the finest craftsman.

He made his way over to her, his eyes flicking over her in a quick but thorough appraisal.

"It was my housekeeper who informed me you'd already made your way into the village square."

"I was impatient," she said with a light laugh and a twirl.

"You look vividly…exquisitely beautiful."

Oh! Everything inside her contracted with pleasure. "Thank you."

"It is a blessing of a sort you have that small overbite."

Theo spluttered, and he chuckled.

"Come, let me take you about."

Her entire body prickled with the awareness of how close he stood. A strange nervousness churned through her, and with a smile, Theo slipped her hand into his.

Sebastian was becoming accustomed to the lurching of his heart whenever Theodosia laughed. Something she'd said earlier had caught at his mind and burrowed deep. Trust his sister a little…and the worry would abate. He had lingered for over an hour in memories and all the ways he had taught her to be careful. He'd realized that he still saw her as his small, helpless sister who needed him to fight all her battles and make her decisions for her when she was a grown lady on the cusp of marriage. The reckless impetuosity of her current actions aside, Perdie was indeed astute and clever, sensible enough to use his name and power to incite the fear of God into any reprobate who might accost her on her journey.

For tonight…he would worry less. Tomorrow began planning anew.

The drums had started to beat, mixing with the fiddlers. "I've never been to a fair before," she said, smiling engagingly at him. "It is so very lovely and lively!" She strolled about, watching the villagers, stopping at the different carts buying pastries and beads she might never wear. The sun had lowered in the sky, but several large bonfires roared, providing light along with lanterns and streaming ribbons. There was also a pole richly decorated with garlands and ribbons. The villagers danced around the maypole, holding and entwining lengths of brightly colored ribbons. The very air itself was festive with laughter, ribald jokes, and music.

Theo ate roasted mutton spitted on a stick, licking the grease from her fingers.

"Your appetite is a bottomless pit."

She grinned. "Not bottomless. I am halfway satisfied."

"You've eaten three meat pies, and now this roasted mutton."

She licked her bottom lip and made a purr of pleasure. "Hmm, and I can smell roasted pork on the air and something sweet. I shall have those too." Using her finger, she tore off a chunk of meat and pushed it toward his mouth.

Sebastian parted his lips and took the meat. Flavors exploded on this tongue, and he chewed thoughtfully.

"Hmmm?" she said with an arch of her brow and a lift of her chin.

"It is very good."

Her eyes danced with merriment. "What creature are you? This is more than good; it is divine."

Sebastian chuckled at her enthusiasm, tugging her further onto the lawns and closer to the dancing couples.

"There was a time if I wanted to eat two pieces of cake at luncheon, I was reprimanded most severely," she said, wrinkling her nose at him. "Everything was moderated by mama, especially how I ate. Apparently, if I am not careful, I will get plump. I held that belief throughout my brief marriage. Existing at the will of others feels remarkably like a stone weighing your body to the bottom of a lake, and there is no chance to push it off and come up for air." Theo stopped, lifted her chin to the sky, and her mouth curved. "Now I eat whatever I want when I want it."

Theodosia stared at the dancers, a wistfulness in her gaze, a touch of longing that pulled at a chord deep inside Sebastian.

"Do you wish to join them in dancing?"

"Oh, yes, though I've never danced around a maypole before. But first, I must try this local ale!" she said, dragging him toward the cart set up advertising their finest ale.

"I've had it before," he cautioned. "It is very strong."

That bit of knowledge did not deter her, and she walked closer to the merry villagers who evidently delighted that a lady and a duke joined their raucous fun. She sent him a teasing glance from beneath her beautiful lashes. "What Sebastian has done…Theo can do."

How incredibly young and lovely she looked. She lifted the tankard the ale keeper had handed her and impressed him by taking several gulps. "It is a fair today. We must drink and be merry!"

He stared astonished when she sampled four mugs of ale in quick succession, humming her delight. "Let's dance!" Theodosia gracefully pirouetted away from him, merriment dancing in her eyes. "Are we to dance, Sebastian?"

The villagers filled with excitement and alcohol roared their approval when he moved toward her, grabbed her about the waist and swung her into the fast jig.

"Oh!" she gasped, grinning. "Challenge accepted."

He twirled and spun her with increasing vigor as the drums pounded louder, and the fiddlers increased their pace. Those who were best acquainted with Sebastian would be astonished at the ease with which Theodosia made him laugh. Many of his friends often lamented his serious nature, but he hadn't known how to be as laid back as his friends when he'd assumed such a large responsibility at the age of nineteen. Seb had tried to balance both worlds, university studies and frivolous pursuits expected of men of leisure and wealth. The duty of caring for his bereaved sister and mother, ensuring the lands and holdings he'd inherited flourished, had dominated his young life. Seb had found purpose and honor in fulfilling his duties and hadn't lamented his lot in life but thrown all his determination into ensuring his family and those dependent on his lands were well cared for. Theodosia brought out a need to laugh and live. Odd. But it was there, under his skin, a burning need to bask in her smile and kisses.

"Whatever are you thinking?" she asked, laughing, almost breathless from the fast reel.

Inexplicably I like you.

"I am not sure I can tell you."

Pleasure lit in her golden eyes. "Oh, a secret! I like those. I am not very good at recalling things when I am tipsy. You can tell me. I won't remember in the morning," she teased.

"Ah, so the lady does know she is foxed."

She flushed prettily. "I concede, the ales were very strong."

Bloody hell, I really like you.

She was quirky and opinionated. Many ladies of his acquaintance would have affected false modesty. Theodosia was a quaint little thing, living to the beat of her own music.

"Mi…milady," a lad stammered, coming up to them, crushing the hat in his hand.

She whirled to face him, smiling brightly. "Yes?"

"Would ye…would ye partner wif me in a dance round the maypole?"

Theodosia dipped into an elegant curtsy. "It would be my pleasure, my good lad."

The young man looked fit to burst at the seam with pleasure. He held out his arms, and Theodosia handed her mug of ale to Seb without sparing him another thought. She placed her hand on the lad's arm and skipped off to join the other revelers. Seb grinned, captivated by her glee. He knew not one lady of his acquaintance who would have honored the village lad in the way she just did. Many ladies would have been offended he dared ask. He leaned his shoulder against the massive oak tree and lifted the tankard of ale to his mouth while he watched her. She appeared flushed and radiant. Their gazes met, and she winked.

The drums beat, the fiddles lifted in the air in an invigorating melody. The villagers gathered around the maypole, and they danced, Theodosia in the thick of the revelry with them. Those who watched on the sidelines clapped and stomped their feet to the music, shouting their encouragement and enthusiastic approval. The torches and the bonfire burned low, and the moon peeked from the clouds. Several couples scuttled away in dark places to steal brazen kisses. The fiddlers played and sang, the villagers drank and danced, and Sebastian never once took his gaze from Theo.

He watched her, and he'd never seen a lady freer and happier. When she laughed, she did it with her whole body, tipped her head to the sky, sometimes pressing her hands against her chest. Something powerful inside of him shifted, and he felt as if he was falling…except he didn't know exactly what he was falling into, never having felt like this before.

She danced and laughed until sweat glistened on her skin. Sebastian couldn't stop watching her. A pretty lady danced up to him and crooked her fingers at him with a sensually teasing smile. A quick glance revealed Theodosia scowled at him, and he grinned. He declined to dance, bowing courteously.

Theo came over to him, looking beyond his shoulders as if she expected to see someone else with him. "Oh la! And where is your lady love?"

"I have no lady love," he said with a touch of amusement.

"I saw a most beautiful lady trying to get you to dance," she groused. "I can be very possessive, you know."

Now this was interesting. Ale had delightfully loosened her tongue. "Can you?"

"Hmm," she murmured, swaying closer. "I am crushed you did not dance with me."

"Have you forgotten our earlier reel? You are foxed."

"I beg your pardon?" she asked with crisp dignity, lifting her chin. "I am nothing of the sort." Then she dissolved into giggles.

He touched the softness of her cheek with the back of his hand. "You appear so delightfully mussed and improper."

"You sound as if you approve."

I do, very much. "Let's get you home."

She pouted. "So soon, it is barely dark."

Night had painted the land in muted shades of gray and pockets of darkness. A quick reach for his timepiece and tilting it to the light from the bonfire revealed it to be closer to 8 pm. Early yet, but his charge was delightfully tippled. They started to walk home through the well-beaten path in the forest. The beat of drums, violins, and laughter sounded in the distance, and she sighed happily. Then stumbled. His lady was well and truly foxed. She swayed again, and he caught her, steadying her with a hand on her hip.

Theodosia reached up to touch the corner of his mouth with a forefinger. Every muscle, nerve and pulsing vein in his body instantly responded to the vision of flawless beauty Theodosia presented with her smile and red cheeks. She was dazzling, breathtaking, her heavy golden blonde hair gleaming in the shimmering moonlight.

"I miss the taste of you," she said, moving that finger to trace the full of his bottom lip. "Do you miss the taste of me, Sebastian?"

He bit back the groan rising inside his chest. He couldn't explain the full gamut of emotions he was feeling toward her just now, but there was a lot of hunger within the midst. "You have been my own brand of torment these several days."

"I am not sure why, but I do like the sound of that. I have been dreadfully annoyed with the constant thought of kissing you again and again. It was very stupid to have kissed you by the seaside. My curiosity has not been satiated but awoken forcefully." With a twist of her lips, she blew a limp tendril away from her forehead.

A tender feeling stirred inside him. "I suspect

you wouldn't have told me that without being soused."

Theo chortled, utterly unperturbed and slapped at his chest playfully. "Who's soused?"

When she attempted to walk away, she wobbled a bit. Her grip tightened on his arm as she sought to steady herself. Seb grinned, went before her and stooped slightly. "Hop on."

"Onto your back?" she whispered, scandalized as if anyone else could hear them out here in the woods.

"Yes."

Her soft weight fell against him, and her slim hands encircled his throat. Some faint scent clung to her, a teasing hint of lavender…cinnamon. Theodosia was lushly curved with a body made for carnal pleasures, and Sebastian wanted to eat her up. He could feel the ache of wanting her deep in his bones. "Try not to strangle me," he muttered.

She giggled against his nape, and he hefted her onto his back, scandalously hooking her legs at each of his hips over his arms. How perfectly she fit against him! Her dress rode up to her knees, and her white stockings gleamed under the moonlight. His next breath was full of her fragrance, the softness of her hair, the sweetness on her breath, the soap she'd bathed with.

It was going to be a long night.

CHAPTER FOURTEEN

*S*ebastian needed to get her back to the cottage and into her room before taking a swim in the lake. He unerringly followed the route across through the trees that brought him out onto the road a short distance beyond the village's square. Seb started back to his manor through the well-beaten off-track running along the estate park wall.

"You are very strong," she said approvingly, slipping one of her hands from around his neck to squeeze a bit of his shoulders. "I suppose dukes have to be strong."

He grunted something unintelligible. It was bloody hard to think when she touched him so. "I suppose so."

"When you are tired, Seb, let me know. We'll switch, and I'll carry you a bit of the way," she murmured sleepily.

"Have you ever lifted anyone on your back?"

She rubbed her face against his nape. "What man has done...ladies can do."

Sebastian chuckled.

"Why do you laugh?"

"I am imagining the spectacle of you trying to lift a man of my size onto your back. I would flatten you to the ground immediately."

A quite indelicate yawn sounded. "You'd roll so that I land atop you...and then perhaps you'd ravish me senselessly."

He stumbled a bit at that and silently cursed. Theodosia tugged a longing inside him that he preferred not to acknowledge. To want another with such acute intensity made Sebastian feel as if he did not know himself, and that was an unpleasant notion, for he had known the kind of man...duke...and father he wanted to be since nineteen years of age.

She nuzzled the side of his neck. "I like you."

"Why?"

"You argue with me."

"And that made me likable, did it?"

"Hmm." she pushed forward to dip her head down over his shoulder and kissed his cheek. Sebastian almost stumbled. "Yes. I stood toe to toe and challenged you many times, and you did not try to dismiss me as inferior. But crossed wits with me. That and your lovely mouth makes you entirely likable."

"Tell me more," he invited.

"About?"

"My mouth…what have you been thinking about my *lovely* mouth."

She all but purred into his neck. "That sinful bit? Too scandalous to share."

Now he was bloody curious. "I thought we were friends?"

"When did I say so? And not even Prue and Charity, I would tell this," she whispered in a shocked undertone.

"So, your musings are wicked then?"

"Very wicked," she said conspiratorially.

The affection in her voice struck him, and he did not think it was the ale. It was entirely possible their liking was mutual.

"Do you like me, Theodosia?" he murmured.

"Yes."

He almost faltered at the surety of her answer.

"You are not at all uncompromising or boorish. A tad arrogant, but that is to be expected. You are very kind and a wonderful lover. You are very likable, Your Grace."

Suddenly it felt absurd that he hadn't known her before this. If not for Perdie's folly, he might have missed ever getting to know the woman he carried, and that felt like a travesty.

"Am I too heavy?" she whispered. "You've slowed down."

"No," he said, hitching her legs a bit higher onto his hip.

A happy sigh and another snuggle into his neck. He trudged along the path, amusement rushing through him when she started to sing.

"Will you not even spare my ears?"

Her gasp of affront had him chuckling, and in retaliation, she nipped his ear. The sensual sting had him pausing and centering himself against the rush of need.

"Where are you taking me?"

"To your bedchamber."

She yawned indelicately. "How excessively boring and entirely disagreeable of you."

"You need sleep. I believe you will be thankful in the morning."

"Sebastian?"

"Hmm?"

"Perhaps we could watch the stars a little bit. I spied the most delightful garden earlier, but I did not get a chance to explore it. Will you take me there?"

He felt a strange clutching at his chest. "This is something you've longed to do?"

"Hmm, but I do not fancy being in the dark by myself. None of my friends ever dared to sleep outdoors with me." Her hands tightened a bit around his neck. "Papa always took out George... my brother to stargaze."

"But not you."

She made no reply, and he did not push her, simply taking the path that led to the immense and well-tended gardens at the southern section of this estate. Once they arrived, he gently lowered her down and opened the wrought iron gate.

Theodosia inhaled deeply, glancing about the gardens. "Oh, it smells remarkable even if we can hardly see it."

They only had the stars and moonlight to guide them. Holding her hand, he guided her through the maze of shrubbery and toward a wide-open area with well-tended lawns. Seb shrugged from his jacket and spread it on the grass. With a wide grin, she tumbled down with a gusty sigh, staring up at the sky.

"Do you know the constellations?"

He lowered himself beside her. "Some. I have a telescope back in Maidstone."

"Why are you sitting? Are you afraid to lie beside me?"

Bloody hell!

"I need your chest as a pillow of sorts, so if you are going to act skittish, that will not do."

A quick glance showed she laughed at him. Her eyes were wide with humor, and she had tugged off her gloves, tossing them carelessly onto the grass. Somehow, she had also toed off her shoes, and now her stocking-clad feet swished across the grass as if she were unable to stay still.

She stared up at him, an unfathomable look in

her eyes. "I do not want to mistake the significance of our friendship. Is it safe for me to rest against you…and watch the stars a bit?"

His heart stuttered, and he loosed a slow breath. "Always."

A faint blush spread across her cheeks, and the smile she gave him was the prettiest he'd ever seen. Sebastian lay beside her, and immediately she curled into his arms, shifting so her back was against his chest, and so the top of her head perfectly fitted into the crook of his neck.

"There is no beauty like the night," she said softly. A trembling sigh left her and then even breathing. She had fallen asleep.

Sebastian stared at the night sky, the beauty of the stars, wondering what she meant to him. He had only known her a little under two weeks but had conversed more with her than several ladies for the last few seasons. He shifted her slightly, so her head was pillowed into the crook of his arm. She was warm and soft and relaxed with sleep. The fragrance of her perfume drifted through his senses, stirring his heart to beat faster. What was it about her that aroused his senses so effortlessly? He rubbed his cheek against the silkiness of her hair, liking the feel of her curved into his side.

Would another fit so perfectly?

CHAPTER FIFTEEN

*T*heo's lashes fluttered open to see the night sky peering down at her. She was pillowed against a very powerful chest, which rose steadily and evenly. The duke slept. The air was dense with the fragrance of springtime flowers, and even then, the flavor of Sebastian's warm woodsy scent filled the air around them. She felt devilishly alive, and Theo felt acutely aware of her own body.

I dare you…

The whisper of her friend's voice wafted through her thoughts. They had started daring each other to reach for the desires in their hearts because mere wagers would not do. A dare wasn't about money like wagers, nor something they encouraged each other to ignore. A dare was about the fulfilling of wishes, hunger, and desires, and they had all sworn never to shy away from dares, especially if they were shrouded in truth. Yet she had ruthlessly suppressed Charity's dare in the days she traveled with the duke, and the desire to kiss him had transformed into something more…

Now she desired to hear how his day had been if only to sit for hours and listen to his voice. She loved conversing with him, and she enjoyed his quick wit, even if it could be dry and skewering at times. She liked the way his mouth curved when he smiled, and she liked the way he stared at her when he thought her occupied.

Theo rolled over, shifting so she lay on his chest, peering down at him. His dark blue eyes were framed by black lashes and slashing brows. She couldn't deny his sinful, obvious beauty, yet it was not the reason being near him made her heart yearn. There was something about the duke…

She touched the tip of his aquiline nose gently. She felt achy and unsatisfied, the dream of kissing him floating away like wisps of smoke. "Why won't you spare me, even in my dreams?" Theo whispered, an ache of such hunger rising inside that her fingers trembled.

Sebastian's eyes opened, and his beautiful gaze ensnared her. She started to lower her hands, a fierce pounding going through her heart. He caught her hand, his thumb smoothed over the soft skin of her inner wrist.

"You have not spared me either, Theodosia."

The touch of his finger at her inner elbow felt like it opened up pathways of sensations within Theo. "I recall that I am your own brand of torment." Before he could reply, she softly said, "I thought you asleep."

"With your dreadful snoring?"

She choked on a horrified laugh. "I do not snore!"

"How would you know? Has a lover told you?"

Sebastian's steady, heated gaze told her how much he wanted her.

Theo allowed her lips to smile even though her heart trembled. "I've never had a lover." *Until now…*

The duke stared at her solemnly. "Never?"

"Never," she whispered.

His gaze sharpened as he evidently turned her words over. "Your husband?" Sebastian queried carefully.

As dismaying as it was for her to admit, she said, "Our marriage was never consummated. The viscount once mentioned that he married me to recapture the feelings of youth. My presence in his life was to flatter his vanity."

The duke went still beneath her soft weight. "You were married for five years?"

"Yes."

"It must have been lonely."

"There were parts of it that were lonely…but oddly, the viscount was a friend of sorts. I stayed in the country to escape society's wagging tongue and only saw him a few times. There were rumors of his vices, of course, and they reached my ears in Hertfordshire. Whenever we met, he treated me with cordiality and also left me a handsome widow's portion." She leaned in so their noses almost touched.

"How long have we been sleeping out here?"

He stared at her, his blue eyes somber. "Ten minutes at best."

Exhaling softly, she confessed, "I am telling you this now so that you will understand the inexperience I touch you with."

He made some strained noise. "You'll be touching me?"

She pushed her face into his throat and breathed deeply of him. "Oh yes…"

"*Fucking hell.*"

His raw curse pulled a smile to her lips.

"Theo—"

She pressed three fingers over his mouth. "And I am not foxed."

He lifted a hand to cup her cheek, and she noted his gloveless fingers trembled. The Duke of Hartford. Trembling. For her. Theo knew it with every part of her. Her heart skipped into an uneven cadence. She turned her face into his hand and kissed his palm. How many lonely nights had she spent longing for a taste of pleasure? Someone to touch her with tenderness, someone to hold and to be held in return? She became aware of a low, warm ache inside, and suddenly the night seemed alive with sound and sensation. The awareness of what she was thinking shook her, and heat blossomed through her entire body.

Theo lowered her head, finding his mouth with her own. She slid her hands through the thick silk of his night-dark hair and caught his mouth with hers. Within an instant Theo felt consumed with arousal. She parted her lips, and their tongues met in a sensual slide. He licked along her lips, then inside her mouth with erotic sensuousness, pulling a ragged moan from Theo.

Sebastian rolled with her, placing her beneath his body, bracing above her on one of his elbows. He framed her face with his other hand, kissing her most thoroughly. Theo couldn't help moaning. She had imagined what bedding entailed many times, but nothing could have prepared her for the sensual reality of being ravished by Sebastian. She breathed slowly and evenly, trying not to allow herself to be entirely consumed with want…with hunger.

Her breasts were swollen, the tips sensitive. There was a strange ache between her thighs. She made a small, strangled sound against his lips when his hand moved down to her throat, his thumb flicking over her fluttering pulse.

He eased from her.

"I am going to undress you."

Something warm and tender shifted inside her chest. "Yes."

A shiver worked through her when his thumb dragged along the inside of her thigh, taking her dress up.

"I'll not remove your stockings and garters."

The gown was now at her waist. Theo gasped when his fingers found the hot flesh between her thighs. His knuckles brushed over her sex, she whimpered, and he swallowed the sound. They kissed deeply and for unending minutes. She was dazedly aware of him taking the dress up and over her head, of his hands untying her tapes and removing her chemisette while he ravished her lips. His mouth on hers was hard and fierce and urgent and wonderful. Sebastian kissed her repeatedly, worshiping her lips, her cheeks, and her throat.

He eased her back against his jacket, and it was then Theo realized she remained clad in only her stockings. She blushed, grateful the dark hid her reaction. Sebastian pushed to his feet, removed his boots and then his clothes. She watched him, eager to see any part of him, conscious of the empty feeling lingering inside. The darkness hid him from her, and she could only listen to the rustles as he completely removed his garments. He stepped from the pocket of darkness, and the pale moonlight shone on him.

"You are beautiful," she whispered.

He was lithe and corded with smooth muscles,

full of power and elegance. His cock throbbed, long, thick, and more intimidating to her virginal senses than she would like to admit. He came down to her, Theo's heart pounded, and her hands trembled as she reached out and touched him, trailing her fingertips over his chest. Sebastian cradled her against his chest. The full contact of his broad chest against hers, the feel of his body and heat completely enveloping her was most incredible. He kissed her thoroughly with his sweet, clever mouth, and she responded with wantonness.

His fingers teased over her belly and down to the space between her thighs where she was hot and damp and throbbing. Two of his fingers stroked deep, sending her senses careening at the dual bite of pain and pleasure. "Sebastian," she murmured against his lips, clutching his shoulders.

"You are so incredibly tight," he breathed raggedly. "I'll need to get you wet…"

"I am ready," she said, trying to pull him closer.

"Not yet; I need you soaked. So wet my cock will slide in easily."

His mouth trailed fire over Theo's skin, the curve of her neck, the slope of her breast, the soft skin of her stomach. And even lower. Then he was there, removing his fingers and replacing them with his tongue.

He was licking her *there*. She felt robbed of air. "Sebastian?"

He sucked carnally at the nerve-rich nub of

flesh. Theo slapped a hand over her mouth to silence the scream. Despite the coolness of the night air, Theo burned, sweat dampening her body. Another lick…a nibble, and Theo went breathless, the flash of fire in her belly arching her hips off the grass. Arrows of exquisite sensation shot through her at every lick and kiss against her sex. She hadn't known this was possible, that such pleasure could be had. Pressure built in sharp spikes, and she instinctively reached down and thrust her fingers through his hair. Her thighs trembled, and her breathing labored. She lost count of the number of times he brought her to pleasure with his wicked tongue.

Tiny moans and whimpers, raw, needy sounds of lust escaped her when he pushed first one, then two, then a third finger into her wet, aching sheath, stretching her sex, filling her, readying her for his penetration. There was pain…but also a deep, unfathomable pleasure as he worked his fingers in and out, deeply, and slowly until she writhed under his sensual assault.

He released her from the tormenting pleasure of his mouth and rose above her. She widened her legs, cradling his weight between her thighs. He fitted perfectly. Theo could feel the fine tremors of his body where his chest pressed against hers.

"Your mouth…your quim…your body is one to savor," he murmured, reaching between them to fit his cock against her softness.

He slid in inexorably, and Theo arched under the harsh yet erotic impact of his penetration. "Sebastian," she gasped, her fingers digging into the muscles of his shoulders. "That was not easy!"

Her sex ached and burned despite her wetness. He brushed a kiss across her mouth, murmuring soothing nonsense, then he was kissing her again, fanning the flames once more. He moved, and she moaned at the tight feeling of his hardness dragging against her softness. Despite the ache…it was also glorious. Breaking her mouth from his, she told him so.

"I want you…feel as if I cannot get enough of you." Sebastian's harsh whisper filled her ear as he drove inside her, burying himself in her aching sex with a fierce hunger.

Theo moaned against his mouth. "I want you too…so much!"

Every deep stroke of his cock as he buried himself in the depths of her body was another shock of ecstasy that made Theo crave more. A sobbing moan was wrenched from her throat as the pressure became too much…and then unexpectedly, she broke apart. Her entire body convulsed, clamping tightly onto his still-thrusting cock. He hugged her closer to him, his thrusts speeding as his own climax followed swift and fierce.

He eased back from her, and their eyes met. Sebastian pushed a sweat-dampened tendril from her forehead. Theo laughed, utterly enthralled with the warm afterglow pulsating in her body.

"The night is getting colder," he murmured, pressing a fleeting kiss to her mouth. "We should return in."

Giddy delight washed through her. "No…you'll keep me warm."

The look in his eyes as he searched her face was hard for her to decipher. But it did not feel cold or distant. It felt warm…sensual. Sebastian eased from her, and she contained her gasp at the ache. He fished around his pocket and retrieved a handkerchief which he used to tenderly clean her.

"I was reckless," he said, his touch lingering on her belly. "I might have got you with a child just now."

The surge of longing that went through her shocked Theo. She should have been frightened.

He touched her face lightly. "I'll be more careful next time."

It was the promise of an affair, nothing more. At her silence, a subtle tension invaded his body. "Do you want there to be a next time?"

"If I say no."

His fingers curled into the grass, but what she saw of his face remained carefully composed. "I'll honor your decision."

"There'll be many more," Theo whispered.

And then his mouth was on hers, and Sebastian was kissing her desperately as his arms came around her. Suddenly, it seemed absurd, unimaginable that she could continue existing in a life where he was not a part of it. *Love me*, she silently cried to him, hugging him to her body and kissing him back with feverish passion. *Love me…for I am falling hopelessly in love with you.*

CHAPTER SIXTEEN

*S*ebastian gently eased Theodosia's head from his shoulder, shifted, and peered down at her. Her mass of hair had been loosed from the chignon and spilled over her naked body like a shower of silken curtains. He admired the erotically flared curves of her hips and the rounded globes of her buttocks. He was tempted to lower himself and bite that firm flesh.

"Control your urges," he muttered. Sebastian had already taken her outside with the stars looking down at them. The next time would not be outdoors. She deserved a bed, slow kisses, and a long night of loving instead of the way he had ravished her. The memory of her passion and how they burned together almost pulled a groan from him. He stood and redressed as efficiently as possible. He would return for her clothes and shoes.

Very slowly, he bundled her into his coat and gently lifted her into his arms.

She murmured sleepily.

He pressed his mouth to her temple. "Shh, I've got you. I am taking you inside."

Theodosia remained sleeping, but a sweet, sensual smile curved her lips, and she snuggled deeper into his arms. Dawn would soon arrive, and he needed to get her into the house before any discovery. Though unlikely with his skeleton staff, Seb still needed to proceed with caution.

Holding her close, he made his way through the gardens and into the house. It was late, and the staff was thankfully abed. He took her up the stairs and into her assigned chamber, placing her on the center of the bed. Drawing the blanket to her chin, he tucked her in.

"I am not wholly conversant on how to conduct an affair," she murmured, sitting up in the bed.

In the act of turning away to leave, Sebastian stilled, then faced her.

The dim light provided by the low burning fire in the hearth revealed only a faint impression of her expression. *An affair*. Was that what they were about? Or did she want more…something more honorable and long-lasting. Did he want more? Where did he really envision her in his life? A mistress? A friend and occasional lover? Discontent filled him at that notion. What then? A wife?

Hell. His heart jerked a harsh beat. "Are you asking my intentions, Theodosia?"

Her lush mouth curved into a smile. "I am asking if I am to sleep alone."

He padded over to her, and she swung her leg over the edge of the bed and sat up. Sebastian leaned down and kissed her. It couldn't be helped. He kissed her with hunger and then with aching gentleness. "I do not wish to define our relationship," he said against her mouth. "For I do not fully understand what I feel for you."

She lifted a finger and traced the outline of his brows, the slope of his cheekbones. "We are lovers," Theodosia whispered. "Do not assume because I was a virgin I want more. I enjoy my freedom."

An unexpected and unbearable aching weight settled against his heart. "Are you saying if I should offer for you my suit would be rejected?"

A startled laugh escaped her. "*Are* you offering?"

"No." *Not yet.*

Shadows shifted in her eyes. "Perhaps I would."

"Why?"

"Because a husband…especially one of your eminence, would try to clip my wings. I am free to do as I please as a wealthy widow."

"You speak of your club." As a duchess…or the wife of any lord, she would not dare keep such a club operating under her largesse. Theodosia lived to her own beat, alive in a way many others were not. The duty of marriage and the expectations of a husband would stifle her dreams and freedom. A burning curiosity drove him to ask, "Do you not dream of a husband…of children? You are incredibly young."

She touched the corner of his mouth with hers, and he wrapped his arms around her.

"Of course, I do," she murmured against his mouth, shifting a little on the bed. "I have yet to find a gentleman who would fit perfectly into my life."

Fuck. Those wry and soft regretful words wrenched through his heart. Was she saying that he, as a duke, had no part in her life? What the hell was he thinking? The odd emotions tearing through him felt nonsensical. Sebastian took a long breath, trying to gather his wits and his logical sense. He already had a list of eligible ladies to select from for his wife. Theodosia was his lover…perhaps eventually his mistress. He would keep it simple and uncomplicated.

Foolishness…for she was the antithesis of simple and uncomplicated.

SEVERAL HOURS LATER, Sebastian stared at his lover, observing the nuance of her expression. Curled by the fire in the library on several plush throw blankets, they had been playing chess for almost two hours. She was a brilliant player when she suffered no distraction. After tasting her mouth about a dozen times, she looked tousled and rosy. He loved her hair, and at his request, she had left it to flow over her shoulders and down her back. Today she smelled of roses. He wanted to splay her on the carpet and lick her all over. It astonished Sebastian how much he wanted her, considering he had made love to her twice more in the long night past. "Checkmate," he murmured, moving his knight into c3.

Her lips parted on a silent gasp, and she sat up, the hem of her blue day dress pushing scandalously up her shin. Of course, she was without shoes or stockings. Sebastian never imagined he could enjoy staring at bare toes. Hers were exceptionally pretty, and he was tempted to nibble at one. It would probably shock her silly if he acted on the impulse. He chuckled when Theodosia tossed a piece from the chess set at him.

"What poor sportsmanship is this," he drawled mockingly.

She narrowed her eyes at him. "You cheat!"

He huffed out a breath, not quite a laugh. "Careful, I might challenge such an affront to my honor."

"Do you deny it?"

"Of course! My honor is beyond reproach."

"Then what were those kisses in between our moves," she demanded in an undertone, throbbing with outrage.

"Kisses, of course. Are you addled?"

197

She surveyed him over the rim of her glass which was filled with sherry. After taking a demur sip, her lips curved, and her eyes glittered brightly. He wondered if that smile was for his benefit. Perhaps not. She was plotting some diabolical revenge upon him for his distracting kisses.

He lifted his glass to his mouth and gave her a look of mocking inquiry. "What are you plotting?"

She was nibbling on her lower lip and, for all appearance, seemed like she attempted to solve a complex equation.

"I was wondering how do lovers behave. I want to explore your body and was wondering how to get you out of your trousers. I am new to these sorts of dalliances. Do I just demand it…or must I seduce you from it?"

Sebastian choked on his brandy.

Her laughter was beautiful, wild, and rich. "I love that I can startle a man of your self-assurance and grace."

"What a shocking want of delicacy."

Sebastian, observing her blush, said, "I tease you."

She sniffed. "So, you've learned the art then."

He pushed aside the chess set and tugged her into his arms. Sebastian cupped her cheeks, lifting her face to his. He kissed her slowly and deeply. When had he become so obsessed with her taste and those soft murmurs of pleasure she made?

He broke his mouth from hers. "You're delicious."

"It's the sherry." She touched his mouth. "Whenever you kiss me, it feels as if my stomach lifts and then falls away. Then an ache settles in… low in my belly. I never knew a kiss could wreak such wonderful sensations. I wonder if this is true for all kisses."

"Are you by chance daring to wonder what it would be like to kiss another?"

She giggled against his lips. If Sebastian were not careful, he could find himself steadily craving her.

"Are such curiosities not normal amongst the *ton*?" she asked with laughter lurking in her tone.

A fierce surge of possessiveness shook him. "You are forbidden."

She turned her face into his throat to take a deep breath of him. "Are you forbidden as well?"

There was an indecipherable emotion in her voice, and he turned it over in his mind. He recalled the many scandal sheets which had been happy to mention Viscount Winfern leaving his new bride in the country to take his mistress to Dover. The sheets had ridiculed the young viscountess for failing to secure her husband's attention, placing the blame for his weakness, disrespect, and inconstancy at her feet. They had taken pleasure in mocking and cutting her for this perceived flaw in character. Sebastian only recalled it, for his mother had mentioned it often and had deliberately omitted to invite the young viscountess to her annual and most sought-after ball.

Sebastian placed a finger under her chin and lifted her face. "Not all men are led by their cocks."

"A most unusual turn of phrase."

"But you perceive my meaning."

"Yes," she said softly. "Not all gentlemen are cads and libertines."

His fingers tightened on her chin. "Anything I ask of you, I would also give in return." He stroked the small of her back, warm and firm and soothing. "As long as we are lovers, you will have my fidelity."

She slipped her hands around his neck, tugged his mouth to her. "And you'll have mine, Sebastian," she whispered achingly, then kissed him with passionate urgency.

A rough laugh jerked from him when she hooked one of her legs around his hip and climbed his body. He slipped his hand beneath her buttocks and hoisted her legs to his waist. He stumbled with her to the wall by the fire, pressing her back against the cool surface. Sebastian couldn't explain the hunger tearing through his body. It was as if he wanted to consume her. Without releasing her mouth from his desperate kisses, he reached between them, opened his flap, and released his aching cock to press his hardened length against her already wet entrance. He thrust, and a wild cry of pleasure sounded from her lips at his deep penetration. Theodosia wrapped herself around him, arms, and legs, kissing him deeply, then whispering for him to move faster…deeper. Her hands roamed over his back, twisting his shirt as her pleasure rose.

He drove inside her harder, deeper, one hand on her hip holding her still, while he used the other to stroke her pebbled nipples. Theodosia bit into his shoulder to muffle her cries as she rose higher and higher. Her wetness bathed his cock in a fiery rush, and he groaned at the exquisite feel.

"I'll never get enough of you," he muttered harshly against her lips. "You are like a drug."

Only when Sebastian felt another ripple of tightness and heat around his shaft did he allow himself his own gratifying release.

A knock sounded on the door.

"*Bloody hell!*"

She muffled her giggle into the front of his shirt. He pulled from her and tucked himself into his trousers. He found his handkerchief and handed it to her. Anyone with sense would see that she had just been thoroughly ravished.

"Come back another time," he commanded.

"It's the duchess, Your Grace."

He froze. "I believe it to be news from my mother." Sebastian padded to the door and opened it slightly. The housekeeper seemed flustered. "Your Grace, the duchess has arrived with guests. It seems they were passing nearby and lost a carriage wheel due to the inclement weather."

"I will be there shortly."

She bobbed a quick curtsy. "Yes, Your Grace, I've put them up in the drawing-room and have called for blankets and refreshment."

The housekeeper withdrew, and he turned to face Theodosia, who had moved from the floor and now sat curled into the chaise longue.

"My mother is here, along with unexpected visitors. They lost a carriage wheel. The blacksmith in the village should be of help, but they might need to be put up for the night."

She glanced toward the window, which showed the rain still sleeted outside. "Do you think the duchess has news of Perdie?"

"I will find out."

He went over to her, framed her face between his hands and kissed her. "I will return soon."

She arched a lovely brow. "Do you expect me to hide here?"

The question jolted him. "No, but you are delightfully mussed. Make your way to your chamber, ring for a bath, and then join us."

She searched his face. "And how will you explain my presence."

He kissed her nose. "With the truth. I kidnapped you."

Then he turned and walked away, pleased with her laughter.

CHAPTER SEVENTEEN

*A*n hour after Theo slipped from the library and ran upstairs to refresh herself, she strolled down the hallway to the drawing-room. She had donned a rose-colored dinner gown which flattered her figure, and Molly had styled her hair in an elegant chignon. Staring at her image in the mirror, Theo had thought her cheeks were too rosy and her eyes too bright. But there was nothing to do about that. She had always worn her emotions on her sleeves, and her mother's constant rebuke had not changed that over the years.

She was falling in love with the duke. Or perhaps she was there already, considering the way she ached to be with him, to touch and to hold. Her steps faltered, and she closed her eyes briefly. It felt improbable that she owned such emotions for him, but she did, and how wonderful it felt. Coming off the last step of the stairs, she turned down the hallway and stopped. The duke walked toward her. The cool, unsmiling, and very arrogant way he looked suggested something was amiss. It had been a while since she spied this uncompromising countenance upon him. "Is something wrong, Your Grace?"

She could feel the color rising hotly to her cheeks. It felt wrong to call him so after the wicked intimacy of last night and only a short hour ago in the library. Theo did not want him to perceive that her belly was knotted with nerves. The corner of his mouth twitched—a fleeting, humorless smile that brought her no reassurance. Had he gotten terrible news about Perdie?

"Your Grace?"

"You appeared very ducal just now. Is it Perdie?"

A shadow moved in his eyes. "She has been recovered."

Theo gasped. "That is most wonderful!"

"It seemed when she left the cottage, she got an attack of conscience and made her way to Maidstone. Instead of sending a letter, my mother hastened to inform me of the good news. Since society had no notion of her missing state, the scandal has perhaps been averted."

She looked behind him at the closed door. "Is Perdie here?"

A muscle flexed in his jaw. "It seems I am somewhat an ogre in my sister's eyes. She was too afraid to face me, so my mother came alone. Our Aunt Millicent remains in Maidstone as a chaperone in the event her feet decide on another flight of fancy."

She lightly touched his arm. "You and your mother must be so terribly relieved she is well and safe."

"We are."

Theo grinned. "I am so happy…" another realization came on the heels of her happiness. Whatever they had between them had ended. She searched his eyes. Was that why he seemed so reserved? She tried to pull her disjointed thoughts into some semblance of order. "I suppose I am to return home while you visit Maidstone."

He stepped toward her, exhaling audibly. "You'll go nowhere. Theodosia, I—"

The door opened behind him, and the duchess framed the doorway, appearing startled to see them there in the hallway. "Oh dear," she said, looking between them. "I was not aware you had another guest in residence."

He stepped to the side and turned so that he could see the duchess. "Mother, may I introduce Viscountess Winfern."

Shock flared in the duchess's eyes before a mask of polite curiosity settled on her still handsome face. "I was not aware you were acquainted."

Theo dipped into an elegant curtsy. "It is a

pleasure, Your Grace. The duke and I are new acquaintances."

Tinkling laughter came from inside, and Theo sent him a quick questioning glance.

"It seems Lady Edith and her mother, along with a cousin, were traveling through Kent, and they lost a carriage wheel. They were fortunate to cross paths with my mother on her way here."

Theo's heart jerked a hot, painful beat. "Your fiancée?"

"I am not affianced to the lady."

"I apologize for giving credibility to gossip," Theo quickly said, hating that she flushed.

"Well, it is not yet announced, but there is an attachment," the duchess interjected, her gaze sharp between them.

A heavy sensation entered Theo's belly. Of course, he would marry Lady Edith; they were eminently suitable. Theo felt silly to even feel the ache in her throat. What she had with him was a dalliance. A very wonderful and wanton one, but the duke would not consider her a suitable wife. He had all the consequence of a ducal title and the holdings; she had been the daughter of a country squire who had married up. A man like the duke would only ever marry a lady with the best pedigree that society demanded. And a woman of Lady Edith's beauty and accomplishments would be a grand societal match.

"There is no attachment," the duke said drily.

Theo made a noncommittal sound, doing her very best to appear unconcerned.

"I urge you to join us for dinner, Lady Winfern," the duchess said with a tight smile, clearly annoyed with her son's stance. "I am very curious as to how you are here. I admit I gave no credit to the rumors my son left a ballroom with you a couple weeks ago."

"Lady Winfern is my guest, mother; that is all that is needed," Sebastian said with icy civility.

All traces of the warm, sensual lover had gone, and in his place, only the duke stood. Theo was uncertain what to make of this transformation. The duchess pulled herself together, forcing a smile to her lips. It was evident he had displeased her with his remarks, but Sebastian displayed an unaffected bearing.

They entered, and Lady Edith glanced up from where she sat before the pianoforte. Her eyes widened with surprise to see Theo, and she shared a quick frown with the marchioness. Another lady sat close to the window, fanning herself though the room was not overly warm, turning an amiable enquiring gaze upon Theo. Perhaps in her early thirties, the lady was quite beautiful, even if a little haughty in her countenance.

Lady Edith was the picture of perfection in a light lemon dress with a golden ribbon tied around her high waist. Her hair was drawn taut and piled atop her head, setting off her face to its best advantage, and all her smiles were for the duke. Quick introductions followed, and it was evident everyone was curious about her own presence in the duke's home. Theo swallowed her groan. This was going to be a terribly long night.

Dinner proved to be an uneventful affair where Theo deftly fielded probing questioning from the marchioness and sly insinuation from Lady Edith. The cousin, Lady Shore, spent an inordinate amount of time trying to find a common interest between Lady Edith and the duke.

The duke enjoyed swimming; Lady Edith had sea-bathed once in Worthing. How charming it was that they both liked the waters. Theo had bit into her lip to prevent her snort. The duchess was rigidly cordial but keenly watched every interaction between her son and Theo. The duke included her in his conversations, and Theo replied pithily and with vague interest. After arching an imperiously questioning brow, he left her to her own musings.

After enduring dinner, they withdrew to the small parlor where Theo was prevailed upon to play music at the pianoforte. She did this gladly, pleased with the distraction from her rioting thoughts. Theo missed a few keys, creating a discordant jangle when the duchess laughingly asked Sebastian to dance with Lady Edith.

"We cannot let such pretty music be in vain," the duchess cried.

Lady Shore hurriedly added her encouragement and a lovely song to accompany the music.

"I do not believe I've seen you dance in years, Sebastian, do indulge your mother."

The duke received this explanation with obvious skepticism, but he obliged his mother.

The marchioness smiled at them. "Your son did appear at a particular ball last season and only danced with my Edith. Quite a stir they made."

The marchioness and the duchess looked on the couple dancing beautifully in the parlor as if they were at a ball. After suffering several pointed glares from the duchess, one thing became starkly clear—the duchess appeared deeply charged by Theo's presence. It was evident to Theo what had happened. The rumors had exploded in London, and knowing where the duke was, the duchess had hurried down with her friend to save her son from Theo's clutches.

A raw ache bubbled in her throat as she watched them. Though the duke's expression was carefully composed, their beauty as a couple was undeniable. Lady Edith glowed, and she stared at the duke with undisguised admiration and longing. Theo couldn't bear looking anymore, so she peered down at the pianoforte keys as she played, ignoring the trembling in her fingers and the ache rising in her heart.

The next day the air was warmer and the sun a bit brighter. No rain clouds lingered in the sky this spring morning; however, Theo's mood was quite blackened. Theo nocked the arrow into the bow with a scowl and aimed it at the straw target several feet away. She drew the bow with all her strength and allowed the arrow to fly with precision. With a thunk, it landed where she aimed.

"That is your arm," she muttered, thoroughly irritated with the image of the duke and Lady Edith dancing. "How dare you hold her so close to your body!"

Selecting another arrow, she let it loose, satisfied where it landed with a harsh *thunk*. "And that is for kissing her hand when you bid her goodnight." Selecting another arrow, she went through the motion of nocking it, then let it fly, slamming the target.

"You, violent woman," a voice rich with soft incredulity said by her temple. "Who is this creature you've shot in the arm…the leg…and in the heart?"

Theo made a low sound in her throat when arms wrapped themselves around her from behind. "I was only aiming for your hands and foot."

"Ah…so the straw is me."

His low laugh, even one that was mocking, sent a flush of pleasure through her.

"I am hoping it is not so serious since you did not aim at my heart."

She sniffed and did not answer him, feeling silly for her jealous mood. The man behind her was not hers; he was simply a fleeting pleasure in the life she'd carved for herself.

"What has you out of sorts?"

"I did not like seeing Lady Edith in your arms."

He stilled behind her, and they stayed like that for several contemplative moments.

"You'll not see her there again," he said solemnly.

Though relief writhed inside her chest, she did not feel particularly pleased with herself. "Though I do not like it, I have no right to feel as I do. It is silly!"

"You are my lover. You have every right. The notion of you in another gentleman's arms, even if it is to dance, is causing my eyelid to twitch. So, my sweet, you are not alone in your madness."

Theo smiled. He was outrageous.

"Where did you learn to shoot so well? Your club?"

"Growing up in Strafford, my favorite pastime was archery. Once I dressed as a lad to enter a local competition and won a fat piglet as my prize."

"Ah…and how was the piglet?"

"Succulent."

There was a pulse of silence.

"You ate the pig?" he asked in mock outrage.

Theo laughed. "To my mother's annoyance, Peggy was my friend and remained a true, muddy friend until I was whisked away to London for social polish and to land myself a titled husband."

Finally, she turned in the cage of his arms and looked archly up at him.

His gaze searched her face. "I missed you at breakfast."

"I could not bear to come down!"

Her outburst seemed to astonish him as much as it did her. Lowering his head, he pressed his lips to hers in a slow, languorous kiss. A hot shiver pulsed through her belly. Theo almost sobbed against his mouth. How easy he made her want him. *Was this goodbye?* She couldn't help noticing he made no mention of the next step in their unorthodox relationship. Would they continue being lovers? Or had their brief affair ended abruptly? Worse, Theo did not know what she wanted. Or for how long she wanted to be with the duke.

She pulled her mouth from his, breathing raggedly.

"Whatever can you be thinking, to bring such color to your cheeks?"

"That I'll miss being your lover. Perhaps it will not be so extraordinary for us to be friends."

"Ah, so you are ending our affair."

She stared wordlessly up at him. "How long can it continue for?"

"For as long as we wish it, days…months… years." He brushed his thumb over her lower lip. "I am not ready to let you go, Theodosia. I feel like we are just beginning. Why are you thinking of ending it?"

A breath shuddered from her. "What explanation did you give for my presence under your roof?"

Arrogance settled over his handsome features like a cloak. "I owe an explanation to no one. Who dares question me?"

How certain he was of his place in this world. "So, no confession to your dastardly kidnapping," she whispered, hating that she was uncertain in confessing she wanted more. *So much more*. Unable to communicate the longing bursting forth in her heart, she tipped onto her toe and mashed her mouth to his in a wild kiss.

Their passion flared too hot and too bright. Before Theo knew what was happening, Sebastian had her back pressed against a large willow tree and her dress bunched at her waist, and his delightful weight was between her thighs. There was a tug on her drawers, and then Theo felt a heavy, hot invading pressure and then he was deep inside of her.

"I love how wet you get for me," he said in a guttural groan.

Weakness infused her limbs, and dark, wanton need seared through her. Their coupling was fast, fiery, and deeply satisfying. Not even a minute later, the tight coil of pleasure expanded through her and with a muffled wail against his mouth, Theo came with a sudden explosion of passion. With a few harsh pumps, he followed her in climax.

Theo laughed against his mouth. "This is madness. We are out in the open!"

"I confess no one has ever debauched me in quite this manner."

He pulled from her, and she winced at the tender ache between her thighs.

"I hear laughter," Theo gasped, peering over his shoulders.

She hurriedly fixed her clothes and patted her hair, testing her chignon still held. Since she could not see anyone, perhaps…

"What is going on?" a voice close by demanded.

Any faint hope that they might not be discovered perished.

It was the duchess.

Theo swallowed her groan and breathed a soft sigh of relief when Sebastian ensured he kept her hidden with his broad shoulders. He gave her time to tidy her hair before he turned around. The duchess's gaze sharpened, and her lips flattened with clear disapproval. It was then Theo noted Lady Edith by the duchess's side. By this time, Lady Edith took in every detail of Theo's appearance and how close the duke stood. The lady was most displeased.

The duchess cleared her throat. "Sebastian, I did not expect to find you here with Lady Winfern."

Sebastian smiled, except it did not reach his eyes. "As you can see, we are shooting arrows. What brought you to this side of the cottage?"

"Lady Edith and I were simply strolling. She is a delightful girl with the most amusing anecdotes."

"Ah, shall we continue walking together?" the duke said.

The duchess gave him a pleased smile. Instead of joining them, Theo excused herself, pleading a mild headache from too much exposure to the sun. She hurried away, feeling everyone staring at her back. She would remain the duke's lover for as long as possible, but it was time to leave this perfectly peaceful cottage. Arrangements needed to be made for her immediate return to London and to her ladies. Though Charity and Louisa were capable of running the club in her absence, Theo missed everyone dreadfully.

She glanced back and faltered. The duke and Lady Edith walked ahead while the duchess remained a few paces behind. He would eventually marry, and Lady Edith was a clear choice. Theo swallowed down the ache. *Do not be silly. It is not as if I want to marry him.* No, to be his duchess, she would most certainly have to give up her lady's club. Not that he would ask her! But what if he did?

I'd say yes.

She was shocked into stillness for a few moments. "Silly, Theo, what are you thinking?" For a chance at a family so very unlike the one she grew up with…They'd be bound by love and laughter and loyalty to each other instead of mere duty. Would she dare to give up the friendships and her unorthodox family at the club, the family she had come to rely on and loved? What if they should grow closer, and he demanded it of her?

I could not…

Theo closed her eyes briefly. *I am overthinking the matter.* She had truly thought herself beyond the possibilities of such yearnings. Over the years, she had grown to be practical, a lady living in reality, accepting that whimsy was no longer a part of her existence.

Until the duke…

You evoke so many longings within me…

Theo blew out a soft breath and turned around. She'd not think of such matters anymore. They would remain lovers, and when they eventually tired of each other, they would part as friends and return to their respective lives.

Simple…and uncomplicated. Except the stirring hunger in her heart mocked Theo mercilessly.

CHAPTER EIGHTEEN

*S*ebastian pressed a kiss to Theo's brow and tried to slip from beneath the sheets. It was early, not yet midnight. He thought it prudent to return to his chamber and not run the risk of falling asleep in her bed until dawn. Theo murmured sleepily and flung her legs over his hips, pinning him in place.

He'd come to her room right after dinner, leaving his mother, Lady Edith, and the marchioness in the drawing-room. He should have exercised restraint and not made love to her tonight, but they agreed she would return to town tomorrow until they met again. That might be a few weeks while he sorted out whatever was happening with Perdie. At the moment, she merited his complete attention.

Knowing they might not see each other for a few weeks, Sebastian and Theo had been insatiable in their passion, made all the more erotic with him trying to keep his lover quiet. He still had bite marks in his palm to prove what Theo thought about that.

Careful to ensure she remained undisturbed, he unentangled himself and came off the bed. Picking up his trousers, he put them on and shrugged into his shirt. He stood there in the dark, staring at the rise and fall of Theodosia's chest. Sebastian grinned when she tossed and muttered, kicking the blanket from her body. She was a terrible sleeper, and he loved that even in this, she was so delightfully improper.

His Theodosia also had a backbone worthy of a duchess. At luncheon and dinner, his mother had been chillingly pleasant, and Lady Edith and her mother indifferent at best. They had acted as if they owned no particular civility to Theo. She had been amused, and for that reason, he had not rudely tossed the lot from the cottage. Theodosia had a charming, unaffected manner that allowed her to find humor in the sly barbs tossed her way. She was also possessive and did not play coy or hide her jealousy. An odd thing to like, but he enjoyed that about her immensely. She was handsome, amusing, clever, and a caring and giving lover.

Earlier, when she had suggested ending their affair, coldness had suffused his entire body, and he'd felt hollow. He'd had lovers before, and whenever a liaison ended, it simply ended. With her, it was different.

He was logical. He was decisive. Sebastian had always governed himself and his urges with a firm hand. Yet when it came to Theo…he felt helpless against the feelings that knotted inside his heart. *Bloody hell*. He felt like a sentimental fool, and he was never the type of man given to sentiment. He had been fond of his past lovers, but none had ever made his heart jerk from a mere smile.

The possibility of never kissing Theo again, of never hearing her laughter, or of seeing that tenderness in her eyes lanced him like a needle through his heart. *Bloody hell*. He rubbed the spot on his chest that ached like a physical sensation.

"You matter to me," he said, frowning as he stared down at her. A woman like Theo was not meant only to be a lover or a mistress.

Turning away, he discreetly slipped from her room and made his way down the long hallway to his. The room was darkened; the fire had died to embers. The night was not chilled, so he opened the windows to allow a cool breeze inside. Sebastian removed his clothes and went onto his bed.

The frightened pants of a lady had him lurching from the bed.

"What the hell is this?"

He flicked on the gasp lamp, bathing the room in a warm glow. Sebastian stilled at the sight in his bed. The shocking audacity rendered him silent for precious seconds. "Get out," he snapped.

"Your Grace," Lady Edith cried, scrambling from the bed, clutching her nightgown at her throat. She walked jerkily over to him, only to slap a hand over her mouth when she observed his naked form.

The lady swooned to lean against his bedpost, and he made no move to catch her. Sebastian grabbed his trousers from where he had tossed it earlier and tugged them on. Then he was striding from the room.

"Your Grace, please!"

The lady launched herself at him, and he spun around with such vigor, she stumbled back forcefully. This time he caught her from falling, lest the silly chit hurt herself. Lady Edith took the opportunity to twine herself around him like a fucking vine and pressed her mouth to his.

He would throttle her.

His door was shoved open, and conveniently the marchioness framed the doorway. Sebastian was coldly furious. They had dared abuse his hospitality by setting a compromising trap.

"Edith!" the marchioness gasped, growing pale. "Your Grace, what is the meaning of this?"

He reassessed his opinion. The mother seemed ignorant of her daughter's machinations.

"Sebastian!" his mother cried, careful not to look at his nakedness.

Then, of course, Lady Shore appeared and promptly gasped, slapping a hand over her mouth.

"It is the way of affianced couples to let… passion overcome their good senses," his mother said with a tight smile at Lady Shore.

"Yes, quite," Lady Shore replied, her cheeks painfully red.

A tight sensation wrapped itself around his chest and cruelly squeezed. With a scowl he pushed her from him, and Lady Edith ran to her mother and collapsed against her sobbing.

He raked his fingers through his hair and met his mother's regard over the marchioness's head. In her eyes, he spied disappointment. *Hell.* Did she really believe he was a part of this set-up? Whether she believed it or not, the duchess urged Lady Edith and the marchioness from the room with soothing murmurs he could not decipher. Lady Shore dutifully followed, and certain words floated back to him.

"This will be the match of the season…a most eligible alliance."

"It was to be expected, of course, since the duke only danced with my Edith last season."

"We must keep a tight lid on what we just saw, and I daresay this marriage needs to happen sooner than later, so there are no speculations if a babe arrives early."

"What a fucking mess," he muttered under his breath.

Sebastian was not certain how long he stood

there, but a soft sound alerted him, and he glanced up. The duchess had returned.

"I thought you held little affection for her," she murmured. "I am not pleased with your methods, but I offer my congratulation on a well-made match."

Raw incredulity rushed through him. "It was a trap. I did not touch her."

The duchess hesitated slightly. "Does that matter?"

He jolted. The duchess held up a hand before he could speak. "The marchioness and the marquess will accept nothing less than a marriage offer! Honor demands that you render her respectable by marrying her and quelling all rumors."

"This can be contained," he said tightly. "This farce does not need to go further than this roof, and all reputations will remain intact."

"There is no certainty with Lady Shore."

"She is the marchioness's cousin!"

"And a notorious gossip and busybody."

"It does not suffice—"

"Wasn't Lady Edith already on the top of your list? Did you not inform me you are ready to select your duchess?"

Her words slammed into his chest with the force of a hammer. He covered his eyes with his hands, raking his fingers back through his hair. When he glanced at the doorway, his mother had disappeared. Sebastian closed his door firmly, ensuring there would be no more surprise visits for the night. He was thankful Theo had slept through it all.

Theodosia.

He dropped his weight onto the bed, staring at the darkness of the ceiling. Sebastian closed his eyes, not wanting to think of how easily he had been compromised. His mother's logic made sense. He had placed Lady Edith at the top of his list. He had always known her to be cunning and clever, and she was a celebrated beauty.

She was supposed to be the perfect wife for him. So why was he hesitating?

And there it was…golden-brown eyes staring up at him with laughter and tenderness.

"Fucking mess," he muttered, closing his eyes, and forcing his heart rate to slow.

Once rested, he would confront the mess head-on.

THE VERY NEXT DAY, Theo took breakfast with the duchess in the Rose parlor. The informal setting had suited Theo, and she relaxed against a large armchair, sipping a most refreshing brew. The duchess was pleased Theo was leaving, and she gracefully inquired after her health, and Theo politely replied, returning the same courtesies. The duchess did not dislike her, but it was evident she did not like Theo being in her son's presence.

Perhaps she thinks I'm a social-climbing upstart.

"Forgive my bluntness, Lady Winfern; why are you here at the cottage with my son?"

"I was helping in his search for Lady Perdita. I became aware that she was missing, and please let me assure you my discretion in this matter is guaranteed, Your Grace."

The duchess slated her a look of disbelief, and Theo's cheek warmed. Good heavens, the duchess thought her presence to be something of a sordid nature. That perhaps she was the duke's mistress, and he traveled with her to alleviate his…boredom.

"Is that what you, young people coin it these days?" the duchess rejoined with a narrow-eyed glare. "I believe you should take your leave before my son returns from his morning ride."

Shock jerked through Theo. It was clear the duchess expected Theo to hastily scuttle away in shame and to be embarrassed by her criticism. The duchess had the societal power and connections to ruin her, but Theo did not feel in a charitable mood about the duchess's prejudicial behavior. "I believe you should take up whatever issue you have with your son, Your Grace."

The duchess's eyes widened. "You dare!" she whispered in an outraged undertone.

"Of course, I do," Theo replied calmly. "I have done nothing to draw your uncharitable spite, and I am not a wilting debutante or some hapless lady to wilt under your disapproval."

The duchess stared as if she were a monster. The marchioness, Lady Edith, and Lady Shore chose that moment to descend in the drawing-room. Everyone had an air of excitement and satisfaction, which notably dimmed in Lady Edith when her gaze landed on Theo. Everyone sat on the sofas in front of the delicacies laid on the large rococo table.

"Lady Winfern, I have been most curious, and I do hope you'll indulge me. You got married and vanished from the London scene," Lady Shore said, artfully pouring herself a cup of tea. "What brought you back?"

"I've been in London these last three years," Theo said with a spurt of amusement. "Perhaps I was just beneath your notice."

The marchioness harrumphed, and the duchess gave her a considering glance as if just noticing Theo for the first time.

Lady Shore smiled tightly. "Perhaps. I've not seen you much about in the *ton*. I gather you do not socialize in the highest and most fashionable circles."

Theo chose to pick up a tart and bit into the flaky pastry, saving herself the necessity of a reply.

Lady Shore favored her with a hard stare. "I wonder how the *ton* will react to Hartford no longer being on the marriage mart. What are your thoughts, Lady Winfern?"

Theo took another sip of the delightful brew. "I have little to offer on the duke's matrimonial state considering it has no relevance to me, Lady Shore."

"Well, I've never heard so decided a tongue in one so young. Very unflattering," the marchioness said, with a pointed glance at the duchess. "We must return to town immediately to inform the marquess of recent developments. I am certain you are also happy with the news, Your Grace."

Theo was too polite to ask about this news, but she sensed the marchioness wanted her to know.

"It is indeed long in coming," the duchess said with a bright smile. "I would like to hear my son's take on the matter before you hurry off to town. We should leave the matter of announcing to the duke."

"What is there to hear about?" The marchioness demanded. "He and my daughter were caught in a compromising situation."

A sick feeling invaded Theo's stomach. Lady Edith stared at her with a triumphant curl to her mouth. Theo lowered her cup to the table with an audible *click*. That drew everyone's attention to her.

The marchioness cleared her throat delicately. "Many ladies on the marriage mart will be rather furious and disappointed the duke is no longer available. I heard an on dit that suggested even a few widows had tossed their bonnets into the ring!

Outrageous of course, it is best the duke married someone in the bloom of youth, well able to give him his heir and several more children."

Theo supposed she was the old hag who needed the reminder. She had to work at composing her expression into one of ladylike propriety.

Lady Shore tittered. "Dear Edith, I hope I do not embarrass you, but I was most shocked at the scandalous way the duke held you to him. Oh, the delightful passion of youth!"

Pain lanced through Theo—sudden and breathtaking. The duke and Lady Edith had been caught together? In an illicit embrace?

"We are to marry, so it was perfectly permissible for me to visit his room briefly for a private conversation," Edith said, blushing prettily.

The pain was so awful Theo couldn't immediately speak or breathe. "Congratulations," she finally offered.

Lady Edith smiled, lowering her lashes, and blushing prettily. "Mamma, we should wait on the duke to make the announcement."

Theo felt a deep shock winding through her, and she tried to shake it off. They were lovers. *Nothing more*. He hadn't offered or made any promises, and she had known all along he would marry one day. *Just not so soon…*Not only a few days after finding the most exquisite joy in his embrace.

She lifted her tea to her lips, sipping and doing everything to hide the turmoil inside. She had spent last night and this morning laboring under a delusion and hopeless dreams. To think she had been fretting he might ask her to marry him. God, she felt so foolish.

They were interrupted by footsteps in the hallway. The duke entered, his gaze sweeping the room. His eyes lingered on her for a moment, and everyone noticed. Lady Edith clenched her fingers around her teacup, the marchioness's mouth flattened, Lady Shore narrowed her eyes thoughtfully, and the duchess frowned.

Theo stood with everyone and dipped into a quick curtsy. He bowed with exaggerated civility as he returned their greetings. The curve of his lips held a mocking edge, and his expression one of chilling insouciance. She felt like she stood in a well-orchestrated play, and Theo grew more and more acutely aware of the duke's observation. *Look away, please, Sebastian.*

As if he heard her silent plea, his regard averted.

"I believe an announcement to the local papers and a notice sent ahead to London would be most proper," the marchioness began.

Suddenly Theo couldn't bear to be in the same room with everyone. Her throat burned, and tears stung behind her eyelids. She would be terribly embarrassed if she were to reveal her feelings to their avid stares. Theo politely excused herself and hurried from the room. Closing the door behind her, she leaned against it, hating how her mouth trembled.

I must leave right away.

Theo rushed down the hallway and up the stairs. She did not want to see the duke. She did not want to hear his explanation of why he must wed. Theo already understood it, for she perfectly understood the *ton's* working and the power of the ladies below stairs. Honor would demand that the duke wed Lady Edith, and she knew he was a most honorable gentleman.

Their alliance had always been expected, so he would do his duty. She did not want to hear his voice, for she did not want him to ask her to stay despite everything. Theo would be a mistress to no man, not even one she had fallen hopelessly in love with.

CHAPTER NINETEEN

"*T*heodosia."

The sound of her name was only a soft murmur on the wind, but she heard his voice. How could she miss it when it had whispered so hotly in her ears as he brought her to pleasure repeatedly. His voice, its pitch and smoothness would forever be interred in her thoughts, and she would hear his laugh and his teasing forever in her dreams.

About to move onto the first step of the carriage, she stood frozen, part in hope and part in dread. She turned to face him. "Your Grace…"

His gaze swept across the footmen who had lowered the carriage steps, and they discreetly melted away with the coachman. "You meant to leave without bidding me farewell?"

Theo hated that she felt like crying. "Did you wish for me to stay for the announcement of your engagement? We had always meant to be fleeting; there is no reason to muddy the waters further. Wouldn't you agree, Your Grace?"

A smooth mask dropped over his face. Before the duke could reply, Lady Edith bustled outside, a tight smile across her mouth. Of course, they had successfully routed the interloper, and the duke was preventing her departure. Lady Edith hurried to the duke's side, clasped her hand around his arm and smiled up at him as if they were lovers and the closest of intimates.

A great pressure swelled in Theo's chest, shortening her breath. She could not bear the thought of never seeing him again, or that he would marry this woman…take her to his bed, love her passionately and have children with her. Theo stumbled slightly, and to her shock, the duke rushed forward, gently gripping her by the elbow to hold her steady.

"What is wrong?" he asked with urgency, his eyes caressing over her face. "Tell me!"

Theo glanced at where he held her and then pointedly at Lady Edith, who had rushed to his side. The lady viewed with disfavor the manner in which the duke held onto Theo.

Sebastian took a deep breath, lowered his hand, and said, "Allow me to call for the doctor."

Theo looked quickly into his eyes, which were intently staring into hers. She wasted very little time in considering what his concern might mean. "I am quite fine, Your Grace."

Still, he studied her, his face shadowed.

"It is but a slight headache from being caught in the rain a couple days ago. It is nothing to alarm a doctor about. I shall be quite fine."

He stared at her as if he were trying to pierce through her soul, and she helplessly returned his stare. The memories of their time together leaped between them, and she almost sobbed at the emotions tearing through her. *Stiffen your spine*, she fiercely reminded herself. He had made no promises. She had asked for none. And he had been well and truly caught in a compromising position with a lady he'd always intended to marry. What was there for her to be sad about?

"I will deal with matters here and call upon you in London."

Lady Edith gasped, her face mottling.

"I am not certain we have anything to speak about, Your Grace."

A muscle tic flickered in his jaw, and Theo knew if not for the presence of Lady Edith, he would have hauled her to him and tried to persuade her otherwise.

"If you will grant me a private meeting before you depart, Theodosia."

She was so tempted. "No, Your Grace. Please let me go."

A cold gleam entered his eyes, and she

suppressed a shiver. It was the purview of men of great consequence and wealth to keep lovers with their wives. Not her. She hoped he saw that resolve in her eyes. Her skin felt too tight, and she was painfully aware of his closeness and the hawkish stare of Lady Edith. Dipping into a curtsy, she turned and made her way into the carriage with the aid of a footman. Theo did not peek through the carriage windows when it rumbled off. She did not want to see the duke with Lady Edith by his side, the picture of the perfect couple.

A lump grew inside her throat until it expanded to encompass her entire body. Something dripped onto her gloves, and with a gasp of shock, she realized tears coursed down her cheeks.

How silly I am being! Acting like a pea-goose, crying over the duke.

Theo leaned her head against the squabs and closed her eyes. "At least I dared…and I lived, and I loved…I fell for a duke," she whispered in the confines of the carriage, conscious of Molly's wide sympathetic stare on her.

It was as if with each sway and rock of the carriage, another memory of their time together was knocked loose from a place where she tried to bury it. Her heart squeezed with frightful want. She truly loved the blasted man, and it might take her a lifetime to recover from the pain of not having his love in return.

Theo sat up. *How do I know he does not love me?*

233

"Would it matter if he did?" *Yes*, her heart screamed. She had just left without giving him a chance to explain anything. God, when had she gotten so muddle-headed! Everything she had experienced with him was worth fighting for. And he was worth fighting for. So why was she running?

Sebastian escorted Lady Edith inside, quite aware of her pleased smile. There was a heaviness against his heart borne from the pain he witnessed in Theodosia's eyes. What had she thought? That he would marry Lady Edith and then ask her to continue on as his lover?

It gutted him that she would think so little of his honor. It gutted him that she had refused to hear him out and had walked away.

There is no need to visit me in London.

Fucking hell! He pushed that nonsensical hurt aside. The only thing that mattered to him was that he could not lose her. How could he carry on and marry another, knowing that a part of him he hadn't known existed was forever lost to Theodosia? There was no space to step back and reassess the situation. He was already surrounded by love and in love with her. Theodosia was important to him, and the people in his cottage needed to understand that. Even with Lady Edith looking on, he should have said the words which had burned themselves into his awareness last night.

Trust me a little, he'd silently pleaded, but she had turned and escaped into the carriage. Sebastian would punish her with pleasure for running before hearing what he had to say.

What if it is that she holds no affection for me? If that was the situation, he would soon learn its truth, and he had no bones about kidnapping her. He entered the drawing-room, and all the ladies present beamed at him.

"We need to make haste in settling the matter with the marquess," the marchioness said without preamble. "When will you send the announcement, Your Grace?"

He extricated himself from Lady Edith and sent her a cool glance of censure when she hovered at his side. The lady flushed and made her way over to the sofa and sat down.

Lady Shore, who keenly observed them, said, "Lady Edith is a fine young lady who will make a wonderful duchess."

"Perhaps you are correct in that regard, but she will not be my duchess."

His mother paled. "Sebastian! Have you taken leave of your senses?"

He gave a grim, humorless tug of his mouth. "They are quite intact madam, why do you question it?"

The marchioness had surged to her feet. "What is the meaning of this?"

The duchess stood and came over to him. "You

must think carefully! You were always meant to marry Lady Edith."

He arched an arrogant brow. "According to whom? Society gossips? I walk to no one's beat but my own," he said with icy civility. "Lady Edith played a game to see her caught in my room. Why would I need such a deceitful witch in my life?"

"Do you blame her?" The duchess snapped. "Did you see how you looked at Viscountess Winfern? There was nothing gentlemanly about it! Clearly, Lady Edith thought she had to fight for your affections?"

"Who gave her the right?"

His mother gasped, staring at him with wide eyes. "Whatever do you mean! Pray have a care for my nerves."

Sebastian allowed his gaze to encompass everyone in the room, then enunciated clearly, "Who gave Lady Edith the right to fight for my affection?"

His mother stared at him as if he were a creature she did not know.

"She will be ruined if you do not do the honorable thing," she said stiffly. "She is a darling child, very good-natured with amiable manners. I've always approved of her for you, you know that. Her father was a dear friend of your father."

Lady Edith appeared mortified that her expectations were being shattered.

"I entered my room and found Lady Edith on

my bed in her nightgown. I commanded her to leave, which she did not do. When I turned to leave, she hurled herself at me. Conveniently Lady Bamforth chose that moment to enter with Lady Shore right on her heels. Do you think me a fool who would cede to such deceitful tricks? It would be a disgrace to my honor if I did!"

His voice cracked through the room like a whip.

Lady Shore jerked to her feet. "Lady Edith was gone from her room for hours! Surely you were with her all that time."

No…he had been in Theodosia's arms.

The marchioness wore a look of self-righteous indignation. "My daughter—"

"Needs a firm hand and discipline!" Sebastian snapped. "Respectfully, nothing can induce me to marry Lady Edith. *Nothing*. And that is because I desperately love another. Lady Edith tried to steal my choice. Contemptible, wouldn't you agree?"

The marchioness had blanched, pressing a hand over her mouth.

Lady Edith drew a great gulping breath.

"I suggest you steer clear of my path for the foreseeable future, Lady Edith. If you ladies will excuse me, I have a carriage to catch up to."

"It is raining," his mother cried.

At the same time, Lady Edith said, "You mean to chase the viscountess!"

Sebastian answered neither. He whirled around and faltered into stillness, a roar sounding in his ear.

Theodosia framed the doorway, appearing most lovely and like a drowned rat. She swiped at the rivulet of water down her cheek and gave him a wobbly smile. "Did you plan to chase me?"

"Yes."

Her mouth trembled on a smile, and her eyes glistened with tears. "I came back because I…I wanted you to make your decision after I told you the truth of my feelings."

He took a step toward her, and Theodosia held up a hand, freezing his motions. "I like the idea of you chasing me."

His mother made a choked sound behind him, and Lady Shore gasped.

"I am going to go back outside…and run toward the gazebo near the gardens," she whispered. Then she turned around and ran away. Ignoring the marchioness's muttered gasp of 'outrageous' and Lady Edith's cries asking him not to leave, Sebastian gave chase.

Theodosia held her dress, sprinted through the hallway, and out the door as if the devil were on her heels. She glanced over her shoulders, and when she saw him chasing her, a ripple of appreciative laughter broke from her. She did not stop running, and he did not stop chasing. Out the cottage, they went, through the forecourt and on to the uneven country road. At one point, she stopped, turned, and rushed back into his arms. Sebastian caught her against him and hugged her fiercely. "I had to come back…what did you want to say to me?"

"Are you asking for that private meeting now?"

She laughed tearily. "Yes. I should have stayed and talked with you when you asked me to. Instead, I was running because I was so afraid of what you might say. But I am not a coward!"

"But you came back."

"I did," she said on a sob.

He brushed his lips over hers, as light as a breath. "Marry me. That's what I wanted to ask you."

His Theodosia laughed into his neck, then pulled back to stare up at him in astonishment. "You were never going to marry Lady Edith?"

"Never."

"I'll not give up my club," she cried, fisting his jacket in her hands.

"I would not ask you to."

As if she couldn't help herself, Theodosia kissed him. "You say that because you are not aware of how scandalous we can be," she whispered against his mouth. "They are my family…they…"

"I would never ask you to," he repeated. "We do not speak of it much, but I know what the club means to you."

Her breath hitched on a sob. "You cannot be real. To be your wife means I would be a *duchess*. Such a role will come with enormous responsibility and scrutiny."

"You'll be more than my duchess. You'll also be my friend and my lover."

Something tender and shockingly vulnerable suffused her lovely face. "I love you," she whispered achingly. "If running the club might bring shame to you…to our family, I will step down. I'll never leave my friends, of course, but—"

He placed a hand over her mouth, humbled by what she was willing to sacrifice to walk fully into his world. "You'll be the Duchess of Hartford. You can do whatever you want, except quit your club."

She flung her arms around his neck and squeezed tightly.

"Do not choke me," he muttered.

She giggled, and he hoarded the sound deep inside his heart. "I love you, Theodosia. Now say you'll marry me."

"Yes! I'll marry you!"

EPILOGUE

Five days later…
Maidstone.

"I thought you would have been frightfully angry," Perdie whispered, her mouth trembling with the effort to hold back her tears.

Sebastian opened his arms, and with a sob, she rushed into his embrace. He rested his chin atop her head while she cried and shook in his arms. "There is no need for tears," he said gruffly.

"Oh, Sebastian, I have caused you so much worry and heartache. I know the full of it, how worried you were. Mama scolded me most fiercely when I returned to Maidstone." She withdrew from him and swiped at her cheeks. "I was most ashamed when I reflected on my actions. I…I should have been brave enough to tell you of my feelings."

He considered his sister and also the truth of his

feelings. "It is entirely possible if you had told me I would have insisted you still wed Lord Owen to avoid a scandal. Your feelings as they were might have been secondary."

Her eyes had widened as he spoke. She sent him a painfully hopeful look. "But now?"

"Now, I want to trust you to make the decisions that impact your life. You were unhappy enough to run away from home…from your family. I failed you."

She shook her head vigorously. "You did not!"

"Trust that you can come to me, Perdie. Always. Even if the problem seems insurmountable, come to me. You must think about whether you wish to marry Lord Owen, and then as a family, we'll discuss the next step. You'll not be forced to honor the agreement if it makes you unhappy. However, an explanation must be provided to him. You cannot run from it. Whatever the outcome is, we shall confront it as a family."

Her sudden smile dawned. "Thank you, Sebastian." Perdie rushed to him again and hugged him fiercely.

"There is something I must tell you," she murmured into his jacket. "In my travels…I met someone."

His heart jolted. Clasping her shoulders, he eased her from him, noting the flush on her cheeks. "Perdie?"

"He is a most odious creature who is insisting

that we are married."

Sebastian choked on air. "Married," he repeated faintly.

"Yes." She cleared her throat. "There was a point he obliged me by pretending to be my husband so I could check into an inn. At first, I thought him so charming and affable!"

"He shared a room with you?" Sebastian asked darkly.

A brighter blush reddened her face. "It was *most* proper, I assure you, and the truth of the matter is he did not know my identity. The daft man was… was insisting I belong to him."

Now he understood why she had run back to Maidstone.

"Who is this man?"

"I do not know the truth of it, but he had a Scottish brogue," she said with great annoyance.

Sebastian knew his sister. She was not frightened, more intrigued. He did not know what to make of it, and he would investigate the matter most thoroughly.

He chuffed under her chin. "There is another matter…I will be marrying Theodosia."

Her jaw slackened. "My Theodosia?"

"She belongs to you?"

"Sebastian! I cannot credit it," she said, her eyes glittering with excitement. "Theo and I are to be sisters! Does that mean it will be acceptable for me to return to the club?"

He smiled at her. "The choice will be yours."

Too overcome, she flung herself into the chaise longue with a happy sigh. With a smile, Sebastian left the drawing-room and made his way outside. A lady was in the hallway, taking off a plumed feather hat. A slight smile hovered about her lips, and that was enough to cause his belly to tighten and his blood to surge with need.

As if she sensed his stare, she glanced up, and a radiant smile lit her entire face.

"You came," he said, walking toward her.

"Did you expect less after teasing me with news of a special license?"

He tapped his top pocket.

"Truly?" she breathed.

"We are marrying tomorrow at nine in the chapel."

She leaped toward him and his arms closed around her by instinct. Theodosia tipped onto her toes and mashed her mouth to his. They kissed, a long and languorous embrace which ended at the shocked clearing of his butler's throat.

"Let's take a walk across the lawns," he suggested, tugging her down the hallway. "I miss chatting with you."

"I do have so much to tell!" she said with a laugh. "My dearest friend Charity has accepted the most shocking wager…or was it a dare, but with the best of intentions to climb into a notorious rogue's, Lord Stanhope's, bedchamber!"

Bloody hell…

THANK you for reading **Love me, if you Dare**! You can Pre-order the next book in the series, **Marry me, If you Dare**!

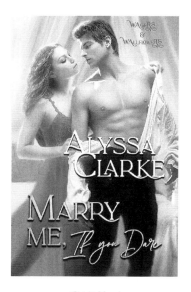

Get it Now!

Reviews are a wonderful way for readers to find new authors. Please consider leaving a review on Amazon or Goodreads, or Bookbub, even if it is just one line know that I appreciate it.

Thank you!

Alyssa Clarke.

ABOUT ALYSSA CLARKE

Alyssa Clarke writes steamy Regency Historical Romances featuring swoon-worthy heroes and sassy, sometimes unconventional heroines! Her debut novel—Love me, If you Dare: Wagers and Wallflowers, came to her in a dream as a hot, fun enemy to lover romance where she played the leading lady who fell in love with a duke who looked remarkably like Henry Cavill.

When not writing, Alyssa enjoys hiking, games/movie night with her husband and two beautiful children, and her Siberian Husky—Cronus. She is a lover of wine, cheesecake, and more wine.

If you would like to keep up to date with my new releases and receive Advance Reader Copies of my books, please sign up for my Newsletter, and follow me on Instagram, Bookbub, and Facebook. I also have a fan group Alyssa's Coterie, that would be fun to join!

You may also check out my website: www.alyssa-clarke.com

facebook.com/alyssaclarkewrites

instagram.com/alyssaclarkewrites

amazon.com/Alyssa-Clarke/e/B08KXHTWG2

Printed in Great Britain
by Amazon